MW01256765

Case of the
Rusty Sword

By

J.M. Poole

Sign up for Jeffrey's newsletter to get all the latest corgi news—
AuthorJMPoole.com

CORGI CASE FILES

CASE OF THE

RUSTY SWORD

BOOK 16

J.M. POOLE

Secret Staircase Books

Case of the Rusty Sword
Published by Secret Staircase Books, an imprint of
Columbine Publishing Group, LLC
PO Box 416, Angel Fire, NM 87710

Book layout and design by Secret Staircase Books
Cover images by Felipe de Barros, Yergen Kachurin, Liana Bedlovska

First trade paperback edition: August, 2022
First e-book edition: August, 2022

* * *

Publisher's Cataloging-in-Publication Data

Poole, J.M.
Case of the Rusty Sword / by J.M. Poole.
p. cm.
ISBN 978-1649140968 (paperback)
ISBN 978-1649140975 (e-book)

1. Zachary Anderson (Fictitious character)—Fiction. 2. Amateur
sleuth—Fiction. 3. Pomme Valley, Oregon (Fictitious location)—Fiction.
4. Pet detectives—Fiction. 5. American Civil War—Fiction. I. Title

Corgi Case Files Mystery Series : Book 16.
Poole, J.M., Corgi Case Files mysteries.

BISAC : FICTION / Mystery & Detective.

813/.54

CONTENTS

ACKNOWLEDGMENTS

My eternal thanks always go out to my lovely wife, Giliane, for putting up with me on a daily basis. Living with a writer isn't easy, I will admit. Your input is always accepted, appreciated, and always welcome!

There are always quite a few people to thank when writing a book. In this case, I'd like to thank my Posse members who helped read for me, including Jason, Carol M, Michelle, Diane, Caryl, and Louise. Then, on the Secret Staircase Books' side of things, thank you to: Susan, Sandra, Marcia, Paula, and Isobel. You all make the finished product so much better! I also need to add a personal shout-out to my niece, Kaylee, who once again helped me create a few characters. This time around, she helped with the professor leading the university excavation team and his two grad students. We'll make a writer out of you yet, kiddo!

I did take some liberties with several of Oregon's universities, so for those of you who have actually attended these institutions, please forgive me if I don't quite get it right. Dates and facts about the start of the gold rush here in Oregon was actually pulled from history, so there's no making that up. And, obviously, the beginning of my state's gold rush started in Jacksonville, which I'm hoping everyone knows by now is the real-life inspiration for Pomme Valley. The town is real, as is the size and location. Also, the layout is exactly the same as I've described it. If you ever get the chance to visit the area, Jacksonville is worth the stop. And, as long as I'm plugging my favorite little town, stop by Las Palmas. Best damn Mexican food this side of the Rockies.

Finally, I'd like to thank you, the reader. With your support, the adventures of our fun-loving trio, er, *quartet* will not be stopping anytime soon! Happy reading!

For Dog Owners Everywhere

Never could I have imagined I would enjoy owning a corgi as much as I do with this one. They're loyal, compassionate, and make great companions. Dogs may only be a small part of our world, but we are their everything, and we truly don't deserve them. If you own one, you'll understand what I mean.

ONE

A ll this time! Think of it, Zachary. All this time, this has been under our feet. Would you want to live in a house with something like this buried underneath? I certainly wouldn't. I wonder who could have done something like this?"

In response, I gingerly poked my head into the large jagged opening in the foundation of my old house. This mystery had literally appeared the same day I had signed my house's death warrant by choosing to have everything demolished. I shook my head.

"I have no idea. Foundations are supposed to be … well, just that: a foundation. Solid. Cement, or brick, or who knows what. But this? Knowing that this house was resting on a hollow foundation for years and years? It would have given me nightmares."

"Do you think Bonnie knew this was here?" Jillian asked.

Bonnie Davies was the previous owner of the land. Actually, she was the previous owner of *everything* here. The house, the winery, the acreage, the … oh, pardon me. I guess I should make the introductions before I lose everyone.

My name is Zachary Anderson, but everyone calls me Zack. That is, everybody but my mother and this wonderful woman currently standing beside me. My wife's name is Jillian, and she owns her own business, Cookbook Nook, a specialty kitchen store here in town. Speaking of which, the two of us live together in Pomme Valley, or PV as the locals call it. PV has a population of less than three thousand individuals, which suggests this tiny slice of southwestern Oregon would barely have a single traffic light in town. Actually, there are three, but that's neither here nor there. If it wasn't for the close proximity of Medford, which is five miles to the east, then I'd probably go crazy living in such a place.

Medford has a population of over eighty-thousand, and as such, has all the popular restaurants, department stores, and even a small international airport, as you'd come to expect in modern-day civilization. Honestly? I couldn't have planned a better area to settle down in, but then again, I really didn't do too much research. I ended up in PV thanks to the aforementioned Bonnie Davies, when she left her entire estate, which included the house, the land, and her private winery, to me and my wife. My first wife, that is.

Samantha, I'm very sorry to say, was killed in a horrible car accident, so that meant I had become the sole beneficiary.

By the way, let me go on the record here and say I have never cared for wine. Every single grape in the world could dry up, thus decimating the wine industry, and I wouldn't shed a tear. Oh, wait a minute. Yes, Lentari Cellars makes a huge profit from the fifty acres of land I currently own, and yes, I guess I *would* be sorry to see that go. But, as for drinking it, nope, it wouldn't bother me in the slightest.

No, wait, that's not true, either. I have found one situation in which I actually like the smell and taste of wine. Turkey Day, and that involves Jillian cooking a turkey by basting it with red wine. Apparently, if you cook the alcohol out of it, then this bottom-feeder is more inclined to give it a try.

Even if I didn't have Lentari Cellars, I'd still be able to make a good living for myself. Prior to owning my winery, I was a romance author. *Am. I am!* I'm *still* a romance author. Wow, where did *that* come from? My book sales used to blow the profits from the winery out of the water, but lately? My master vintner, Caden, has ramped up production of the winery to practically one-hundred percent efficiency—to keep up with demand—and for the first time ever, last month, wine sales edged out my book sales.

One final job I should mention, I have been involved with the police department. No, I'm not a cop, or an employee of the department, or anything like that. Instead, I am a paid consultant. Whenever the local police force encounters a case that has them stumped, I am called in to see if I can shed any light on the subject.

All right, all right, I know I'm not exactly doing a good job being honest with you. The Pomme Valley Police Department really couldn't give a flying fig about my opinion on these strange police cases. Instead, they wanted me to get my two dogs involved, Sherlock and Watson. Yes, you heard that right. There are two four-legged detectives living in my house who have solved so many police cases that it puts the local force to shame.

My good friend, Vance Samuelson, PVPD's senior detective, continues to scowl at me every time I bring this particular subject up. What can I say? Vance and I have an interesting history together, beginning with him arresting me for murder less than twenty-four hours after I first moved to Pomme Valley. I could go into details here, but I won't. That story has already been told.

By now, I assume you have a question or two regarding my two dogs. Well, what can I say about Sherlock and Watson? For starters, they are corgis. Don't shake your head. I *know* you've heard of the breed. They are the short, squat little herding dogs favored by the Queen of England. Yep, *those* ones. Those two dogs have the ability to zero in on things so bizarre and out of the ordinary that you'd think they simply picked up a strange scent and had lost focus. Well, I can tell you I've stared at such a mismatch of items that I've gotten used to simply pulling out my phone and snapping a picture of whatever the dogs are looking at, figuring that even though it might not make sense now, somewhere down the line it will. Therefore, whenever I'm working a case with the dogs, I will usually gather our friends together at a restaurant of my choosing—don't judge, I end up picking up the check—and see what they all think about the *corgi clues*.

For the record, we really don't make too much headway on the case. The significance of the clues is often not realized until long after the case is over. How those two corgis do it, I just don't know. In fact, I don't think I ever will. They're amazing, and I know it. The problem is, they know it, too.

Now, back to the present.

As Jillian and I were staring through the opening made in the foundation, movement in my peripheral vision caught my eye. Watson, my red and white female, had come up to sit beside my left foot, and she was whining. Glancing over at Sherlock, I could see he was moments away from letting out a warning woof, which usually tells me he's picked up on something and that I should really be paying attention.

"What is it?" I asked the dogs. Giving Jillian a lopsided grin, I stooped to pick up Watson and held her up so that she could look into the hollow foundation. "See anything, girl? What has you spooked? There are no ghosts in there, Watson, so …"

"*WOOF.*"

Feeling two paws suddenly applying pressure to my thigh, just above my knee, I knew that Sherlock had reared up on his hind legs, and was imploring me to look down. Shaking my head, I did just that.

"Awwooowooo."

"Two syllables," Jillian reported. "I know if Sherlock let's out a three-syllable howl, that's his *pay-attention-to-me* noise. Four?"

"Four?" I repeated, grinning. "If there are four, then I can only assume he's seriously aggravated with us."

"What about two?" my wife asked, as she pointed at Sherlock. She squatted next to the corgi and draped an arm across his back. "What is it, pretty boy? Do you want to look in the hole, too?"

Sherlock let out a single, piercing bark.

"I'll take that as a big ten-four," I said, as I lowered Watson to the ground and picked up Sherlock. Resting the bulk of my tri-colored corgi's weight on my arm, I lifted him up so that he could look into the opening. "There. See anything?"

Sherlock was silent as he gazed inside. I could hear him sniffing like crazy, as though I had dropped a treat onto a shag rug, and he wasn't going to rest until he had found it. After a few moments, Sherlock twisted in my grip so that he could look back at me. I, unfortunately, was looking through the opening, too, and wasn't paying attention to him. What I would have noticed, had I actually been a little more observant, was that both Sherlock's head, and my own, were now on the same level, and were less than two feet apart.

Sherlock's long snout turned my way, his tongue came out, and just like that, he got my attention back.

"You little booger," I laughed, as I set the feisty corgi down and wiped my face with the back of an arm. "You were just *waiting* to do that, weren't you?"

"See anything good in there?" Jillian wanted to know.

"Well, now that the demo crew has left for the day, and I've got some time to actually look around, I can see that there is some other stuff in there. It looks like an old trunk. There are several crates stacked against a corner, and what looks like a number of medium-sized stones, set in a circle."

"A hearth," Jillian guessed.

"My thoughts exactly," I said, nodding. "Now, if that *is* a hearth, that would mean it was probably used as some type of camp site, wouldn't it?"

My wife nodded. Both corgis had stretched out on the ground and were watching us.

"Why," I began, adopting an exasperated tone, "would someone pour a false foundation around the campsite? Yes, they're trying to hide something, but what?"

"I think you're right, Zachary. There's

something going on in there, and I think we need to figure out what it is."

"And how would you like to do that?" I asked.

Jillian tapped the wall with her finger. "Well, first and foremost, I'd say we need to make the hole a little bigger, so that we can make it inside."

"Stay here. I'll get the sledge hammer."

"Bring a flashlight, too, would you?" Jillian called, after I turned away.

"No problem."

Ten minutes later, with both dogs now on leashes, and with Jillian in control of them, I took my first turn at what it was like to work on a demolition crew. And, let me tell you, it's not as fun as it looks. I'm no expert in physics, but when you take one solid object (a sledge hammer) and whack it against another solid object (the foundation), then what you get are some seriously uncomfortable vibrations traveling through the handle.

"Yee-ouch!"

"Are you all right?"

I inspected the closest wall. "Yeah, I'm good. I really should have brought a pair of gloves. Hey, check it out! We now have a nice, long crack running down to the ground. We can use that to our advantage. One more blow ought to do it."

It took three more, for a total of four, hits. Four lousy swings with the sledge hammer, and what did I have to show for it? Two blisters. On each hand.

"Hand me the flashlight, would you?" I requested. The sledge hammer was set on the ground, so that the handle was leaning against the wall. Snapping on the light, I stepped inside. "I can see where the sword was picked up. There's almost a perfect imprint on the ground here. I don't know who put it in here, but it's been here a while, that's for sure."

"What about that trunk?" Jillian wanted to know.

"Well, let's see. It appears to be covered in leather, and it has several metal bands wrapping around it, like metal ribbons. It has a number of brass studs all over it, too. I guess they're decorative? And, there's one large fastener on the front, acting as a lock. For the record, it looks like it's sealed up tight."

"Oooh, how mysterious!" Jillian exclaimed, delighted. "I can't wait to find out what's in it!"

I noticed a misshapen lump on the ground, near the trunk's bottom-right corner. Nudging the object with the toe of my shoe, I inadvertently let out a grunt.

"What is it?" Jillian wanted to know.

I picked the thing up and shook the dust and cobwebs from it.

"I've seen this type of thing before. Jillian, this is a hat. More specifically, this is a hat commonly worn by cavalry soldiers during the Civil War. I think … I think this might have been some type of camp of theirs."

"From the Civil War?" my wife dubiously asked.

"Well, yeah. Think about it. The sword that was found? I thought it looked like a cavalry sword. Then, we have this hat, which ..."

"Kepi," Jillian interrupted.

"Huh?"

"That hat? It's called a kepi. It's just the style that it is. Do go on."

"Right. All right, this kepi thingamajig was worn by cavalry soldiers, and we have an antique trunk that's probably from the same time. My dear, I think all of the stuff in here is from the Civil War era."

"How exciting! Do you know who's an expert on this kind of thing?"

Curiosity piqued, I glanced through the opening to stare at my wife.

"Who?"

"Burt."

That'd be Burt Johnson, the huge dude who owns and operates Relics & Antiques, a local antique store in PV. And when I say huge, I do mean just that. Burt is—at minimum—six inches taller than me, which makes him at least six and a half feet tall. He also had to have at least a hundred-fifty pounds on me, but not one ounce of that was fat. Ever see those strongman competitions with the guys who casually dead-lift an entire automobile? Or pull a 747 airplane *uphill*? I'm almost positive I've seen someone looking a lot like him participating in those competitions.

"We've already had him do so much for us. Are you sure you want to ask him about this?"

"He works with antiques," Jillian reminded me. "His passion is for old things. Granted, he might not be a Civil War history buff, but I would be remiss if I didn't go to him first."

"You've got me convinced." I automatically scanned the sky, looking for the sun. It was already low on the western horizon, suggesting sunset would be within the hour. "I say you call him tomorrow. Besides, it'll give me time to do some research on my own."

Jillian perked up. "Oh? What kind of research?"

I pointed at the foundation. "I want to find out everything I can about the house. When was it built? Who built it? Was there a previous house before it?"

My wife nodded. "That's a good plan. I'd like to know the answers to those questions, too. What are you going to do about the stuff in there?"

I looked back through the opening in the foundation.

"What stuff? *That* stuff? I don't know. I was going to leave it until tomorrow morning, but judging by the look on your face, I'm guessing you don't want me to do that."

"Let's pull our cars around so we can load everything up. I'd hate to see any of this stuff stolen, now that we're not living here and won't be able to keep an eye on everything."

I shrugged. "Sure, I guess. Why not?"

Once I was back on the same side of the foundation wall as Jillian and the dogs, I took a few steps toward my Jeep when I felt the leashes go taut. Looking down at the corgis, I saw that both of them were back at the foundation opening. Sherlock and Watson were jostling about, looking for the best vantage point to look inside the hollow interior, only they were about two feet too short for that. I pulled a few loose cinderblocks to the ground, thus enlarging the hole. That way, by rearing up on their hind legs, the corgis could look inside.

"What do you see?" I asked the dogs.

Unsurprisingly, neither corgi answered. I did see Sherlock's ears twitch, but that was about it. He looked back at me, snorted, and returned his attention to the scene inside.

"That's probably not a bad idea," Jillian said, as she appeared at my side.

"What?" I wanted to know.

"Documenting where everything was. I think Sherlock might want you to take some pictures."

Looking at Sherlock and then Watson, I nodded. Since neither dog was paying me any attention, I gave the leashes back to Jillian and stepped through the opening one more time. Pulling out my phone, I took pics of everything I could see. Crates, trunk, miscellaneous piles of junk, and so on. There were eight new pictures on my phone after I finished.

I heard a soft snort and the shaking of a collar. Apparently, Sherlock and Watson were satisfied with my attempts at preserving the area and were ready to move on. Jillian had already moved her car, and once she took the leashes back, I did the same.

All in all, it only took about twenty minutes to load the dusty items into our vehicles, and that included me digging out several tarps to try and protect the interiors. With the dogs loaded, I followed Jillian back to Carnation Cottage and we called it a night.

The following day, the two of us drove to Hidden Relics & Antiques. Giving Burt a two-fingered salute as I came walking through the door, I couldn't help but notice the look of alarm that appeared on his face. Why would he be nervous about my arrival?

"I can only assume you've changed your mind about something, Mr. Anderson," the proprietor began. "Just tell me which piece you need back and I can …"

I held up my hands in a time-out gesture.

"I'm doing nothing of the sort. No take-backs, and I mean it."

"Oh. Well, you have me at a loss. What can I do for you?"

Jillian finished parking her car and appeared at my side.

"Mrs. Anderson," Burt acknowledged.

"Hello, Burt. We're sorry to bother you, but we

were hoping you'd be able to help us out."

Swinging my eyes around his shop, I noticed that several of the pieces Burt had salvaged from Aunt Bonnie's old house were now prominently displayed, with price tags on each item.

Burt's face lit up with interest.

"Did you find something?"

I handed the leashes to Burt and headed back outside, stopping only long enough to prop the front door open. As soon as Burt saw me struggling with the large trunk, he quickly passed the leashes to Jillian and came hurrying around the counter. One hand. He scooped up that trunk with one flippin' hand and held it up as easily as if I was holding a loaded plate of food. I could only hope my shocked eyes didn't give me away.

"Mrs. Anderson? Could I get you to clear a section of the counter off?"

Jillian nodded. "Of course."

The two of us worked to move pamphlets, small displays of jewelry, and a box of candy bars that were from the local high school's most recent fundraiser. Burt set the trunk down on the counter and stepped back.

"Where'd you get this?"

I chuckled. "Well, it's a funny story. The foundation to the house that was recently torn down … you know, where you picked up all of the furniture and items you wanted?"

Burt nodded and waited for me to continue. I pointed at the trunk.

"This, and the rest of the items in my Jeep, and in Jillian's SUV, came from within the foundation. A part of it was hollow."

Burt's eyes widened with surprise. He looked at the trunk.

"It's Civil War era."

"A sword was found, too," I said. "It's covered in gunk, and I have it in my Jeep, but I thought the same thing. It looks like it's US Cavalry, so that, along with the trunk there, makes me think these things had been hidden away since, what, the 1860s?"

Burt walked around the trunk a few times. "Wooden, covered with leather here and here, although it looks like it's peeling. Metal bands with brass studs as decorations. There's an oval name plate on the top here, with what looks like a couple of letters. SJ. Mean anything to you? All right then. Moving on. Looks like there's a simple lock to keep the lid closed. Do you have the key?"

I shook my head. "I didn't see one."

Burt walked behind his counter and pulled out a small metal lockbox. Opening it, he rummaged through it for a few moments before he pulled out an old brass key.

"Those trunks aren't the most complex, nor are their locking mechanisms. With a little bit of ... well, I was going to say, with a little jimmying, we should be able to open it, but it wasn't necessary. It just popped open."

Jillian and I crowded close.

"Well," I prompted. "What's in there?"

"Just about everything you'd expect to find in a Union soldier's trunk," Burt said, after gazing inside. Thanks to the counter being around my waist level, and the large trunk—with the lid propped open—reaching a height of around my upper chest, I couldn't quite see inside without rising up on my tiptoes. I'm ashamed to say I could have used a step stool. As for Burt? He was fine. He reached behind the counter again and pulled out a box of nitrile latex gloves. Snapping on a pair, he gently started pulling items out and reverently laying them on the counter.

"Looks like we have a bundle of old maps. They're too delicate to try and open them here. They would need to be properly preserved." Burt reached in again and pulled out a stack of books. "Same for these. Look, I can make out the title of this one: *Wit & Wisdom of Abraham Lincoln*."

Jillian pulled out her phone and was already looking it up.

"It's a book of Lincoln's most well-known quotations. I guess this soldier was a fan of the president?"

Burt nodded. Reaching in for another handful, this time he pulled out what looked like a wad of linen. Placing the cloth on the counter, Burt carefully unfolded several fraying, faded, long-sleeved shirts.

"Well, I'll be. These are linsey-woolsey shirts."

I stepped forward. "They're *what*?"

He motioned the two of us closer. "It means the fabric used to weave this shirt has a cotton warp with a woolen weft."

I looked helplessly at Jillian for a better explanation. When she shook her head, indicating she didn't know what that meant, either, I was about to ask for clarification, but Burt beat me to it. He reached behind the counter and grabbed a notepad and a pen. He then drew a series of vertical lines, close together, on the paper.

"These here represent the warp. In this case, they'd be cotton fibers, all in a straight line like this. With me?"

The two of us nodded.

"Good. Now, to bind the fibers together, a second thread, typically an unbroken one, is inserted either on the left or right, and it is *woven* back and forth."

Burt drew a thicker line, starting at the lower left corner, and moved it horizontally across the vertical lines. Reaching the end, he looped it up and then back to the left, directly on top of the first pass. In this manner, he zigzagged the unbroken line up the vertical fibers he had drawn.

"This second line, the unbroken one, is the *weft*, and was made of wool. This style of weaving has been around since ancient times. Cavalrymen wore linsey-woolsey shirts because they were durable, the shirts kept them warm, and they were cheap."

"Even back then, the government was looking

for the cheapest way out," I scoffed.

"Actually," Burt contradicted, "the government wasn't responsible for purchasing shirts like these. It wasn't part of the uniform. The troops were all responsible for purchasing their own personal items."

I pointed at the shirts and looked around the store. "Do you carry these types of shirts?"

"I have a few blankets that are similar to this."

"But, no shirts?" I guessed.

"None, I'm afraid. I have to admit something, Mr. Anderson."

I looked up. "And what would that be?"

"I'm really starting to enjoy having you walk through my doors. Or me through yours. Can I keep looking?"

I nodded. "Please do."

His body language remained cool and calm, the picture of a consummate professional. However, his face betrayed him. A look of delight appeared on the big man's face as he eagerly reached inside the trunk for the next item. When he pulled his hand out, it could be seen clutching a worn, dark leather bag the size of a purse.

Jillian smiled. "A Coach purse, it is not."

Burt nodded. "It's actually a simple leather bag used to hold … yes, I'm right. Do you see these?"

Burt opened the bag's flap and pulled out two empty metal boxes.

"Cartridge boxes," Burt reported, as he held them up for us to see. "Each is designed to hold about twenty cartridges. These would hold the cartridges and bullets necessary to allow the soldier to engage in combat."

"How do you know so much about all this stuff?" I asked. "I mean, yes, you're an antique store owner, but you haven't really batted an eye anytime you pull something out of that trunk."

"I was a history major," Burt admitted, without looking up from his inspection of the two metal boxes. "My great-great-grandfather fought in the Civil War. When I found his name on a roster, located in the National Archives Building, I was hooked."

"Good for you," I said, and I meant it. "I don't know too much about my family going that far back. I've never really looked."

"One of these days, Zachary, you're going to have to let me research your family tree," Jillian said, taking my hand.

"Deal. Burt? What else is in there? You're the only one tall enough to look inside that thing."

"I can move it to the ground, if you prefer," Burt offered.

Jillian giggled, and I'm sure my face flushed red. "No, it's good. We trust you."

Nodding, the antique dealer reached inside again. This time, he pulled out a medium-sized, fold-over canvas bag. I could see a large, leather buckle on the front and three leather straps on top of the bag.

"It's a knapsack," Burt reported. "Most soldiers

used something like this to carry their personal effects: Bible, canteen, hardtack, and so on. Do you see these three straps on top? They're used to secure a bedroll, or maybe a blanket."

I raised a hand. "Did you say hardtack? What's that?"

Burt nodded. "It was probably the most common meal for a soldier fighting in the Civil War. Hardtack is a cracker-like food made from flour, salt, and water. It could last for days, which unfortunately, meant it was prone to mold."

"I wouldn't want to eat something like that," Jillian decided.

"It was often tasteless, and hard as a brick," Burt agreed, "which was why the soldiers started coming up with different ways to eat it. Let's see what we have in here. Yes, do you see this box? You can see a few crumbs. That'd be the hardtack. And this tin? It held coffee, which is what this soldier probably had to dunk his hardtack into so that he could actually eat it."

"I wouldn't have survived back then," I decided. "Blech."

"If that was all you had to eat, then I'm sure you'd change your mind," Burt argued. "Let's see if there's anything else in the trunk. All right, here we go. I was waiting for this one."

Burt pulled out a small leather pouch which had several loops visible on the back. Carefully unsnapping the front cover, he gently pulled the lid back to look inside. Holding out his hand, and tipping the small pouch upside down, a handful of small brass cylinders, with a single closed end, tumbled into his hand.

"Percussion caps," Burt explained. "They were used to fire the majority of weapons in use during the Civil War. Isn't this something? To think, these caps were in the possession of an actual Civil War soldier."

I nodded. "Crazy, I know. Even crazier was that all this was right under my nose. Literally."

"Have you thought about what you're going to do with all of these things?" Burt asked, failing to hide the eagerness in his voice.

"I haven't, no," I said, shaking my head.

"If you ever want to sell this, *any* of it, please call me first, would you?"

"You're on," I promised.

"What are you going to do with the site?" Burt asked.

I looked up at the shop owner and tilted my head, just like a curious dog would, I'm sure.

"What's that? What am I going to do with it? Nothing, I guess. It's sitting right where my new house is going to be built. The construction crew is anxious to get going, and I have to admit, so am I, so … all right. I'll ask. Why do you want to know?"

Burt cleared his throat and a look of unease appeared on his face. "I was just asking because, well, from the sounds of things, there's a better-than-average chance the owner of these items might still be in there."

Every last bit of color drained from my face. Why hadn't I thought of that? My old house's foundation is the prime example of something that should be properly excavated. What if someone *was* buried in there?

I angrily shook my head. Are you kidding me? Knowing me, and my bad luck, of course there'd be human remains in there. My only saving grace was that there was no possible way I could be implicated of any wrongdoing. I hope.

TWO

The following day, I was hard at work in the spare bedroom at Carnation Cottage. Jillian had been kind enough to let me set up my desk, laptop, printer, and a few other electronic gizmos in her spare room, so I had a private place to work. So, if Jillian was going to check on me, she'd find me seated at my desk, notebook open in front of me, and with pencil in my hand.

However, she wouldn't be, not today. Cookbook Nook was in the middle of a top-to-bottom store inventory check, and with many books and kitchen gadgets calling her store home, it was one place I didn't want to be. Don't get me wrong, I've helped Jillian out before, doing that very thing, but I find it tedious, monotonous, and about as exciting as watching paint dry.

Thankfully, my darling wife had said that she was planning on having her staff help her this time, and since there are now four staff members working at Cookbook Nook on most nights (all were high school students, by the way), Jillian theorized she had plenty of help to do a full inventory sweep *and* keep someone working the registers at all times. Therefore, that meant I was *here*, working on the planning stage of my next book. What that means is, before I'm willing to turn an idea into a full-fledged book, I need to know how the book starts, what type of character development was going to happen, what beats I wanted it to contain, and most importantly, how I wanted it to end.

Now, some authors are able to write without having an outline to follow. Authors call that particular style *writing by the seat of their pants*. Not me. If I tried, it'd be a horrible mistake, and I don't make that statement lightly. After all, I've tried it before, and it was a terrible mess. My mind has a tendency to wander, so if there's not a set outline to follow, I'd never be able to write a book my publisher would be willing to publish.

Therefore, here I was, lost in my thoughts as the events of my newest idea flashed through my brain in fast-forward. No, it would not be taking place here, in the United States. Yes, it would be somewhere in Europe. The gender of my protagonist has yet to be decided. No, I didn't want to make them young, thus making it into a *coming of age* story. However, I would if the right situation arose.

A vision formed in my mind. Green, rolling hills. Lush grass and stone cottages were everywhere.

The native language wasn't spoken by many, and thankfully, English was also an official language, and more importantly, the primary language. The country was small, it was very picturesque, and I'm proud to say, I've been there before. All of us were, if truth be told: Jillian, myself, and both Sherlock and Watson.

Of course, I'm talking about Wales.

Thinking back to the time we were there earlier this year, I imagined a setting much like Betwys-y-Coed, a small village in the Conwy valley on the border of Gwydir Forest. Full of quaint shops, the "Prayer House in the Woods" is a popular tourist destination for many, and therefore, a perfect place to set my story.

I didn't want the plot to be predictable, which meant I needed something other than the tried-and-true formula found in so many romance novels: visiting tourist meets handsome—or attractive—local and falls desperately in love. No, I need something a little more interesting. What about a tourist and a chance encounter with a crook? And, what about making them a female criminal?

The creative juices started to flow. Here was something I could get on board with. Various scenes started appearing in my head, like floating thought bubbles. I took note of each one as it passed by me and added it to my list of beats. Now, I realize that's a strange term for an author to use, but it's one that all writers should be familiar with.

A beat is a moment in time which pushes the story forward and compels the reader to take notice on what might happen next. Yes, that's the technical definition, and I know that because I just looked up the answer online. It's funny, huh? Me, being a writer, knowing *what* a beat was, just not the best way to explain it.

As my list of beats grew, I started thinking about characters. Who was I going to need? I flipped the page of my notebook and started a list. One relatable, somewhat goofy male protagonist (age to be determined) and one wily, intelligent, and attractive con artist. Also added to the list was a local detective sergeant, one highly irritable detective inspector, and possibly a handful of colorful locals. Next up, I needed something for the con artist to do. Why was she there? What brought her there? Was she going to steal something? A piece of jewelry? A sum of money? Maybe an expensive car?

Maybe she was planning on pulling some type of con. Perhaps the visiting burglar stumbles across some type of local legend? No, scratch that. That particular storyline has been used so many times it's not even funny. All right, if not that, then perhaps this tourist was someone who had become separated from a large group? Yes, that sounded good. Maybe this particular person was a quiet introvert and just so happened to have a lousy sense of direction? He could wander off, exploring, got turned around, and doesn't make it back until long after their buses had departed.

Smiling, I hastily scribbled notes as the story began to unfold in my mind. I just had to write it down—quickly—before I forgot any of it. I should know, it's happened to me on more than one occasion.

A bark sounded, from down the hallway. It was loud enough that it succeeded in pulling me out of my (imaginary) trip to Wales and back into reality. Pausing long enough to verify what I had heard came from one of my corgis, and no other vocalizations were forthcoming, I returned to my notebook. Ideas were flowing, plot lines were weaving together, character development played out, and damned if my poor hands could keep up.

Eager to start fleshing out the story, and explore the possibilities that were beginning to present themselves to me, I returned to my notebook, stretched my fingers, and prepared to write. It was times like these where I didn't want to regret coming up with a brilliant idea for a story, but failed to write it down, 'cause I promised myself I'd jot it down later. If I don't transfer my thoughts to paper the instant they appear, then they're gonna end up as a lost cause. I'm sad to say it has happened more times than I'd care to admit.

I was determined not to let it happen this time. Even if my notes weren't the clearest, or not that legible, I was going to get the gist of idea down before the little man upstairs, responsible for filing away information, spun the dial and yet another random idea appeared.

Back home, er, I mean, prior to it being torn down, my old study was on the second floor. I had converted one of my spare bedrooms into an office, with another of the upstairs rooms drafted into service as the dogs' room. However, we were here, in the historic house Jillian had purchased for herself. Carnation Cottage. It had been completely remodeled, decorated as though an interior designer had laid everything out, and was perfect for Jillian.

However, now that the two of us were married, and we had plans to build a mansion on the fifty acres of Lentari Cellars, this house had become unnecessary. Luckily, since I know how much this house means to my wife, Jillian was planning on keeping the house as-is, in preparation for any family member who might need it down the line.

The reason I told you all of that was to illustrate the type of person I was lucky enough to marry. Since my house has been torn down, Jillian very kindly has allowed me to take over not one, but *two* rooms in her house: one for me, and one for *them*. The problem was, they were making me look like a liar at the moment, because they were spending most of their time in the living room, watching television.

Yes, you heard that right. Yes, I know how that sounds. However, if you happen to own a very energetic dog, and in my case, I had two, then you would explore *all* options with regards to keeping those two little furballs occupied. In this case, I had actually found a streaming channel full of programming especially tailored for—I kid you not—your pets. I thought it was a joke at first, but since both corgis had settled down the moment I activated the free preview, and sat there the entire time I had it on, I immediately prepaid for a full year and have been willingly renewing it ever since.

Anyway, the corgis were in the other room, watching their channel, and I had just heard a second bark, which made me think I needed to check on them. Pushing away from the desk, I headed for the living room. Their Royal Canineships were stretched out on the couch. Both dogs looked over at me the moment I came into view, as if to accuse me of being the one who interrupted them. Turning to the television, I caught the tail end of a pizza commercial. Shaking my head, I had just taken a few steps back, to return to my desk in the other room, when ...

"Woof."

"Now what, guys?" Turning around, I returned to the couch and companionably sat next to Watson, who immediately rolled onto her back. Stroking her silky belly, the three of us watched some type of political ad, pertaining to the upcoming elections.

"Woof," Sherlock repeated.

I reached around Watson to give my tri-colored boy a friendly scratch.

"What's the matter? You don't like politics? Trust me, pal, the rest of the country is right there with you. Any time you want to bark at a politician, you have my explicit permission. That goes for you, too, Watson."

I started to rise from the couch, when Sherlock woofed again. Watson then whined. Exasperated, I looked at my two dogs and then back at the TV. Was there something they wanted me to see? Sighing, I humored them by pulling my phone out and snapping a few pictures of the television.

"There, are you happy?"

That apparently did it, because both dogs settled down and returned their attention to the television just as their program came back on. What was the show, you ask? Footage of herding dogs, chasing butterflies. It was their favorite.

"Whatever, guys. If you need me, I'll be back at my desk, okay?"

Like I expected an answer.

As soon as I was seated at my desk, I returned my attention to my notepad, but the momentum was gone. I just couldn't get my mind back on my upcoming project, no matter how hard I stared at my notes. Instead, I found my attention returning to what we found yesterday, and what was currently still in Burt Johnson's possession: the Civil War trunk and the three or four crates found with it.

Did I make the right decision in letting Burt keep ahold of the items? Dismissing my objections, I shook my head. If anyone had proven themselves trustworthy, it'd be him. I would love to see someone try and make off with anything in the big man's possession. At his size, built like an NFL linebacker, there would be no getting Burt Johnson to do anything he didn't want to do, and if you were stupid enough to try and steal something from him? Well, in that case, you deserved to have your head pinched off as easily as us regular folks dead-heading a flower bush.

Thinking back to the foundation of Aunt Bonnie's old house, and how it was currently cracked open like an egg, I couldn't help but wonder if I was making too much out of this. It wasn't like the entire foundation had been hollow, as we had first assumed. It only turned out to be the southwestern corner, and even then, the hidden area was no more than ten by twenty feet in size. Sure, we had found some authentic Civil War memorabilia, but should I have really reached out to SOU to see what I should do about it?

SOU, in case you didn't know, was Southern Oregon University, located in Ashland. They were about fifteen minutes south of Medford, and about thirty minutes from us, in PV. Not knowing what I should be reporting, or who I should be reporting it to, I left a hasty message with the person manning the information desk and was promptly told it'd be delivered to the right people. I just didn't know how quickly an institution like that would respond.

What if SOU wanted to excavate the site? Should I let them? If I did, what would they find? Could Jillian be right, in that there's a distinct possibility human remains could be buried nearby? Again, knowing my luck, that was almost a certainty. Although this time, I couldn't imagine that the local police would try and pin anything on me.

My cell rang. Looking at the display, I grinned.

"Were your ears burning, buddy?"

"Hey, Zack, what's up?"

It was my friend, Vance Samuelson, who coincidentally enough, is the senior detective at the Pomme Valley police department. He and I have a long history together, and even though we started off on the wrong foot, he and his family have become close friends with me and Jillian.

"Tell me this isn't a coincidence. Tell me Jillian didn't ask you to call."

"Jillian didn't ask me to call about anything," Vance told me. There was a brief pause on the phone, and then he chuckled. "But, she *did* ask Tori to ask *me* to ask *you* about what you guys found."

"Hit me with your best. What kind of repercussions am I looking at now?"

"Oh, come on. Do you even know if they're going to find anything?" Vance asked.

"I don't even know if the university is going to call me back," I clarified, "let alone look at what we've found."

"Zack, what the heck are you so worried about? If there does happen to be something in that hollow foundation of yours, then I can guarantee you it was there long before you came to town."

"Yeah, yeah. You know what my luck is like around here."

"I know your luck when you first arrived in town," my friend corrected. "It's not like that now. You've become a town celebrity. Well, your dogs have, anyway. You've got nothing to worry about, buddy."

"Well, that's reassuring."

"Are you being sarcastic?"

"No, sorry. I mean it. That's reassuring. I was literally just asking myself if I was blowing this situation out of proportion by reaching out to the university."

"Tori was talking with me about this," Vance said.

Tori, Vance's wife, is a tall, lithe redhead, and probably the smartest person our group knew, aside from Jillian. She works at the local high school as a history teacher, and from what Vance later explained to me, Tori was chomping at the bit to take a look at the items that were found.

"Finds like this don't happen every day. If there's a chance there are human remains on your property, then it becomes your responsibility to identify the unlucky person and see to it they get a proper burial."

"Even if it's been over a hundred and fifty years?" I asked.

"Especially since it's been so long," Vance

confirmed.

"Yeah, okay. I guess I can see your point. If they do call, I'll give them permission to do whatever they need to do."

"Good man, Zack. This won't delay things with the house too long, will it?"

"Well, I'm told demolition is supposed to take another two days, and then the construction crew can get in there to begin digging out the new foundation. If the university deems the site important enough to send out a team, and seeing how little that area is, I can't imagine it'd take them more than a day or two to look around, dig a few holes, and so on. Oh, hey, look at that. Someone is calling me."

"It's probably the university," Vance told me. "Go ahead and take it. We'll catch up on Friday."

"You got it. Should we hit up Sarah's again?"

"Sarah's Pizza Parlor," Vance said, giving me a surprisingly negative grunt. "They do have the best pizza in town, but we've been there a lot lately. Let's go someplace different this time, what do you say?

"You're on. You come up with a couple of places, and so will I. I'll call you later so we can make the final decision."

I terminated that call and answered the new one. Luckily, I caught it before it could go to voice mail.

"Hello?"

"Mr. Anderson? It's Burt Johnson, Hidden Relic

Antiques."

"Hey Burt, how's it going? Learn anything new?"

"As a matter of fact, I did. I've been able to figure out which regiment your unknown soldier belonged to."

"You did? How in the world did you manage that?" I asked, incredulous.

"Well, I had to identify the soldier first," Burt explained. "And, after having time to methodically search through the belongings you found, I located a name: Private Ernie Howell."

"Where did you find a name?" I wanted to know.

"It was in his personal Bible," Burt answered. "It was one of the books inside the trunk. Mr. Anderson, something like this would be a treasure to that family. With your permission, I'll see if I can locate a living descendent and see if they'd be interested in having the Bible returned to them."

"You have my complete support," I told Burt. "If they want it, they can have it. If they don't, well, you can have it for your store."

"You're too generous, Mr. Anderson," Burt returned. "You've already given me enough. I'll need to find some way to pay you back."

"That really isn't necessary," I began.

"But, it is. Now, with regards to his unit, are you interested in learning what it was?"

"Sure. Let's hear it."

"Private Ernie Howell was a member of the 4th Oregon Volunteer Infantry Regiment, stationed in Grants Pass."

"Grants Pass. To us, that isn't too far away. But, back then, when all they had were horses, that's a considerable distance away."

"I agree."

"His name was Ernie Howell? That's odd."

"What is?" Burt wanted to know.

"The trunk had SJ on it. I just assumed those would be the owner's initials."

"It's hard to say," Burt finally admitted. "They're letters. The meaning could be just about anything, although I will admit I originally thought the same thing, too."

"How'd you find out which unit was his?" I asked.

"I have a contact at the National Archives Building, in Washington D.C.," Burt said. "They were able to take the information I had and match it up to our Private Howell. As you have just said, there was no mention of the 4th OVIR ever stationing itself in Pomme Valley. You're right. It was too far away."

"So, what was he doing here?" I wondered aloud. "They. What were *they* doing here?"

"That's something you'll have to find out for yourself," Burt said.

"No problem," I assured the shop owner. "I appreciate all your help."

"Stop by the next time you're in town," Burt instructed. "I can give all this stuff back to you then."

"You're on. Thanks, Burt."

Hanging up, I had taken no more than two or three steps away from my desk, intent on taking Sherlock and Watson for a little walk, when my phone rang for the third time. Looking at the display, I knew the number was from my state, but it was not from around here. Now what? Do I ignore or do I answer? Shrugging, I took the call.

"Hello?"

"Is this Mr. Zachary Anderson?"

"It is. Who's this?"

"This is Dr. Marcye Wolfe, from the University of Oregon. I'm a professor of archaeology and am assistant curator for the Museum of Natural and Cultural History here, in Eugene, Oregon. I do believe you might know what I'm calling about?"

"The University of Oregon?" I repeated, frowning. "Actually, I didn't call you. I reached out to ..."

"SOU," Dr. Wolfe interrupted. "Yes, we know. They're the ones who reached out to us. They don't have an archaeology department, and wanted to know if we'd field the call."

"Oh. I didn't even think of that. I guess I should've looked that one up online, huh? Great. Now I owe them an apology."

"No, you don't," the university professor assured me. "Tell me, you're in Oregon, too, aren't you? Pomme Valley, is it?"

"I am, yes."

"And you've made some type of discovery which might interest us?"

"I have, yes."

"Tell me about it," Dr. Wolfe implored.

"Sure. Well, long story short, I'm demo'ing my old house, with the intent to build a bigger, newer one. During the demo, a bulldozer started to take out the old foundation, but once a piece had been removed, we were all surprised to find it hollow."

"A hollow foundation?" Dr. Wolfe repeated, clearly startled. "Was this for a residential or a commercial building?"

"Residential," I told her. "It's the house I inherited, which is why I moved here in the first place. I've already looked up when the place was built: 1911. Even then, I think something else was here prior to that."

"What makes you say that?" Dr. Wolfe asked, genuinely curious.

"Well, call it a hunch," I began, throwing some humor in my voice, "but when you find what a local antique dealer calls a veritable treasure trove of Civil War memorabilia, including weapons, personal effects, and even leftover food, then it makes you wonder just how long it's been there."

"Wait. You're telling me you found the remains of a Civil War encampment? And this is on your property?"

"Yes, it's on my winery."

"Ah, Pomme Valley. They *do* have some fine wines coming out of your little town."

"Let me guess. You've heard of mine. Lentari Cellars?"

I heard the creak of a chair and got the impression Dr. Wolfe had just leaned forward and was now sitting up straight in her chair, at her desk. She was probably paying more attention to me, too.

"Ah! Of course! You're Zachary Anderson. Wait. Oh my goodness! Sherlock and Watson? You're their owner?"

"Wow, you, too? It would seem everyone has heard of my two dogs."

I heard a delighted laugh. "Well, who wouldn't? After all, they've made the news several times lately. I'm an archaeologist, Mr. Anderson. You had better believe news of the discovery—and return—of a very important piece of missing jewelry will eventually land on my desk. They were the ones who found it, weren't they?"

"They were," I confirmed.

"And your recent wedding? You held it in Westminster Abbey, in England?"

"I didn't hold it there," I laughed. "The Queen did. It was her present to us, and a reward for our part in the return of … them."

"Say no more, Mr. Anderson," Dr. Wolfe said, lowering her voice. "I know full well what you're referring to. So, this foundation … it's still intact?"

"Kinda. Most of it is gone, but the section that was hollow is still there, minus one corner. The bulldozer created a hole in it when it first drove over. I enlarged the hole enough to step inside. Only two of us have been inside: a construction worker, who was lowered in, and me. The first thing we found was a rusted cavalry sword. I didn't want to leave the other items in there, unprotected, so I took what I could find."

"You didn't do any digging?"

"I did not."

"You do realize there's a better-than-average chance you have human remains at that camp?"

"And *that* is why I was encouraged to reach out," I told the professor. "On the off-chance there is something there, I decided I needed to let someone know about it. So, what do you think?"

"I think you made the right call," Dr. Wolfe said. "You mentioned you were in the process of tearing down your old house?"

"Yes. I have crews waiting to be given the green light so they can finish ripping out the old foundation so that another crew can come in and dig a new one."

"How long can you give us?" Dr. Wolfe asked.

"Oh, gosh, how long will you need? The area isn't that big. The whole foundation wasn't hollow, just a small part of it. I'm guessing it'll only take a few days?"

"Can you tell me how many square feet?"

"Hmm, I'd say it was no more than two hundred."

"I see. Well, in that case, we'd need at least a month to properly excavate the site."

"What? A whole month? Are you serious?"

"To properly preserve that site," Dr. Wolfe

patiently explained, "we would need to dig some test pits, analyze every bit of excavated earth, and if something of interest *does* come up, well, then it would be even longer. Hmm, I'm gathering you're not too keen on the idea of delaying your house for that long."

"Admittedly, I'm not," I finally said, after a few moments of silence had passed. "But, I'm also not going to be the one to refuse you access just because I can't wait."

"Can you give us two weeks?"

I sighed and tapped my fingers on my desk.

"All right, here's what we'll do. I will give you two weeks, but I'd really like to believe it won't take that long. If something happens, and you're able to clear out even earlier, I ask that you guys keep me in the loop."

"Oh, without a doubt, Mr. Anderson."

"One final stipulation. This time frame--it starts tomorrow."

"Perfect," the professor smoothly returned. "I was just going to say that I'll have my team there bright and early tomorrow morning."

"Eugene is nearly three hours away," I recalled. "Your team would have to leave before sunrise."

"If I can arrange for their accommodation," Dr. Wolfe said, "then I'm sure they'll be hitting the road tonight."

"Who are you going to send?" I asked. "Do you know?"

"Yes. The team will be headed by Dr. Steve

Houston, one of our top archaeologists."

"Not to put too much emphasis on this, but is this whole situation … I don't know, *worthy* of an entire team of people to come check it out?"

"It's a team, yes," Dr. Wolfe said, "but it won't be that big. Dr. Houston will be bringing a couple of grad students with him. Ah, there we go. I just received confirmation a local B&B is nearby, and has vacancies."

I perked up. "A local B&B? Can I ask, which one did you choose?"

"Highland House," Dr. Wolfe answered. "Do you know it?"

"Yeah, you could say that. My wife owns the place."

"Indeed? Well, you can tell her Highland House has a very accessible and easy-to-use website, and the rates are more than accommodating."

"I'll be sure to pass that along. Okay, well, I guess I'll see your people tomorrow."

"I'll have them there by 8 a.m. Thank you again, Mr. Anderson."

Hanging up the phone, I looked over at the dogs, who were both watching me intently, their program long forgotten.

"It's done, guys. The university is sending some people out to take a look at what we found. Hopefully, they'll be able to confirm there's nothing there and I'm just someone with an overactive imagination."

As was typical with me, I wasn't even close to

being right. Human remains *would* be found, and it wasn't just one person, but half a dozen. Our new house was going to have to wait for a while longer.

THREE

Bright and early the next day, Sherlock, Watson and I were back at our old house. Well, what was left of it. The rest of the foundation had been broken up and removed, but the southwestern corner, the section that we had all been shocked to discover was hollow? It was the only part that still remained.

As we pulled up to one of the parking spots at the winery's main building, I opened the door for the two corgis and watched them sprint down the hill, straight toward the encampment. Suspecting my two dogs were going to do just that, I casually walked down the hill. This was going to be the location of our brand new mansion, only thanks to this discovery, we were now delayed for an indeterminate amount of time.

Gazing at the vacant area where Aunt Bonnie's house used to be, I tried to picture how the new three-story monstrosity was going to look, sitting next to the winery's main processing building. The plans called for seventy-five hundred square feet, spread out over three floors. Oh, there was also a bonus room above the garage.

The first floor of our new house was going to be the largest, measuring in at over five thousand square feet. It included a grand salon, library, kitchen, and theater (with a small stage!). The master suite was also on the ground floor, and that included a sitting room, his and her closets, and access to the veranda on the back of the house.

Let me pause for a moment. I know exactly what you're thinking. Zachary, did you mention your new house is going to have a theater with a small stage? And I would say … why yes, yes it will. I remember seeing that on the blueprints the first time and turning to my lovely new wife. The only thing I could say was, "At this point, why not?"

Jillian assured me it was one of the features that attracted her to this house's original design. Yes, it's really something, especially looking through the plans for the first time. But, enough of that for now. Time to get the tour moving once more!

Walking up to the second floor you would find three additional suites in the main house, complete with their own bathrooms. There was also an upper dining room, upper library, upper foyer, and upper grand salon. Over at the garage, the second floor has a large living room and two bedrooms that share a bathroom. What did they call it? Jack and Jill rooms? Whatever. Anyway, if you climb the stairs in the northern corner of the garage living room, you'll find a twelve-hundred square foot bonus room.

If I could figure out how to turn that into a retro arcade, I would. However, going up several flights of stairs would make it difficult to get the machines I'd want up there, so we'll have to wait and see. The only way that would work is if I either had some type of ramp installed, which, let's face it, wasn't gonna happen, or perhaps ... I knew what I was going to do. Since there were essentially three levels in the house, I think I was going to have to see about installing some type of elevator. Then again, this didn't help with the bonus room, since that was over the garage, which was in a separate building. Hmmm. Well, it was a problem I was more than happy to tackle at a later date. After all, where there's a will, there's a way.

Now, completing this house is the basement, where you'll find some of the best features this chateau has to offer. First up is the game room, which is located directly below the master suite. Oh, let me tell you something. I'm already trying to find a super-secret way to connect up the master with the game room. Have you seen Batman Returns, with Michael Keaton and Danny DeVito? In it, there's a scene where Michael Keaton reaches inside an aquarium and presses a button, which opens a door to the Batcave. *That*. That was something I would *love* to do. And, if you're wondering what Jillian would think about something like this, well, she'd think I was silly and, in the same breath, would encourage me to do whatever I wanted. I'm still researching different ideas.

Continuing on, the game room also includes a bar with a spot to store a healthy collection of wine. Yes, I detest the stuff, but Jillian enjoys a glass of Chardonnay every once in a while. Plus, we like to entertain, and many of our friends enjoy a glass of wine when they come over. More specifically, they love the Syrah that my own winery makes. Also, of note in the game room area, is a sitting room. This is also where you would find the stairs leading up, to the ground floor.

To the left of the game room would be my pride and joy. I was taking great care to make sure this particular area is designed and stocked with the right furniture and equipment. The theater. It was going to have reclining theater seats that could accommodate twenty of our friends. The screen will probably be close to ten feet wide, by seven or eight feet tall. State of the art surround sound speakers would be hidden inside the walls, with easy access so that I could replace/repair as needed. Same for the equipment. The mech room, for all the necessary technology, would be accessed by a concealed door set into the rear wall. Oh, I'll also mention that the entire basement was going to be professionally soundproofed.

Yes, all of this was going to cost a fortune, but I didn't care.

One of Jillian's favorite areas was next: an

indoor pool. At nearly twenty feet wide, and over fifty feet long, it will be professionally maintained, with the responsibility of all the equipment and balancing of chemicals sitting squarely on someone else's shoulders. It will be heated, with a spa, and also a small sauna, which didn't interest me, but Jillian said she'd love one. On the opposite side of the pool would be a well-stocked gym, complete with exercise bikes, treadmills, climbers, free weights, and so on.

Another staircase leads to the private English garden on the southwest corner of the house. This, I can safely say, *is* Jillian's favorite part of the new house plans. I told her the sky was the limit, so she could design any type of garden she wanted.

I could not wait to begin construction. However, as I approached the corner of the foundation, and I saw the three representatives from the University of Oregon already out of their vehicle, which was a white step van with a big green O on the door, I knew the construction crews were going to be delayed by at least two weeks. More, if they found anything. As Dr. Wolfe had explained earlier, there were three of them and they were headed toward me with looks of extreme excitement on their faces. I knew without a shadow of a doubt that whatever was in that foundation had just messed up my timeline. The university's team were all way too eager, smiling profusely, and anxious to start the excavation, leading me to believe they must have arrived early enough to take a look around for themselves.

Sherlock and Watson arrived at my side first. Did they bark? Did they growl and adopt aggressive stances? Not at all. Both went straight to the person with the shaggy brown hair, wearing wire-rimmed glasses, a blue plaid flannel shirt, and khaki pants. This guy, who was probably in his early thirties, dropped to a squat and ruffled the corgis' fur. Both dogs, naturally, rolled onto their backs and waited for the belly rubs to commence.

"Come on, guys," I complained. "There's dirt on the ground. Show a little restraint, huh?"

The man with the glasses straightened and held out a hand. "You must be Mr. Zachary Anderson. I'm Professor Steve Houston, from the University of Oregon. With me today are Bobbi Campbell and Noah Clarke, my two finest grad students."

I looked at the two students and shook their hands as well. Bobbi Campbell was in her early twenties, had ginger hair tied in a low ponytail, hazel eyes, and a freckled face. Noah Clarke was probably the same age, but then again, he had one of those faces that could be anywhere from twenty to thirty years old. Noah had blue eyes, blond hair, and a smile which probably made the ladies melt. He didn't have movie star looks, but I could tell he was in way better shape than I was. It made me want to ask him how long he had to spend in a gym to maintain such a low amount of body fat. Noah was also an inch or two shorter than Bobbi, which might explain why the male grad student had elected to wear boots with one-inch-thick heels.

"Professor Houston, call me Zack. Down there, rolling around in the dirt at your feet are Sherlock and Watson, who ... you've heard of them, haven't you?"

At the mention of their names, both grad students perked up. Bobbi gasped with surprise and pulled out her phone.

"No, it can't be! Professor? Would these two be the dogs who ..."

"Yep, it's them, Bobbi," Professor Houston confirmed, rising to his feet. "Didn't I mention it? Hmm, must've slipped my mind."

"You know how much I love corgis," Bobbi gushed. She dropped into a squat and gave each of the dogs a thorough scratching. "I can't believe it. These dogs are famous!"

"You're *that* Zachary Anderson," Noah was saying, as he nodded his head. "Pomme Valley, Lentari Cellars, and two corgis. I should've known, too."

The professor chuckled, pulled his students to their feet, and gave each a companionable slap on the back. "Now that you're done fawning over the dogs, perhaps we could get down to work? Mr. Anderson ... er, Zack ... can you show us what you found?"

"I'm guessing you already looked for yourself," I said, adopting a casual tone. "By the looks on your faces as I walked up, I could tell you three were all eager to get going. So, what I *can* do is tell you what

I've removed from inside the cavity."

Professor Houston grinned. "Very well, you caught us. I'm sorry, we should have waited, but we were all extremely curious."

"And now that you've looked?" I asked, looking down at the dogs. "Sherlock. Watson. Get up, guys."

Both dogs rolled to their feet. Sherlock gave himself a solid shake to dislodge any leftover dirt particles.

"I believe a group of people used that area for an indeterminate amount of time," Professor Houston said.

I held my hands up in a time-out gesture. "Wait. More than one person was in there? How can you tell?"

"It's just a preliminary inspection," the professor told us. "We won't know for certain until we start to excavate the area, but I'm willing to wager a tidy sum that my theory is correct. Tell me, what did you find?"

"I'm arranging to bring everything back here so you guys can take a look," I announced, which earned me some appreciative looks from the university's team.

I recounted all I could remember about what had been found, what had been discovered, and I even told them a few theories I had come up with, which I'm sorry to say, earned me a patronizing smile from the professor.

"This trunk," Professor Houston was saying, "do

you think it belonged to a single individual, or could it have been used by more than one person?"

"Based on the contents, I'd say one person. That's why I was so surprised, when you said you thought this little hideaway had been used by more than one person."

"Well, we'll see what we can find. Bobbi, Noah, get out the stakes and string. Let's grid the site and choose a few test areas. Would you two start unloading?"

The students nodded and returned to the van. Several large, black storage containers were offloaded and arranged in neat stacks. Next, the two students pulled out armfuls of long metal poles. Then, what looked like a huge, folded piece of white canvas was placed next to the poles.

"It's a tent," I murmured to myself.

Overhearing, Professor Houston nodded.

"Yep. It's standard operating … wait. I had assumed Dr. Wolfe would have told you about what was going to happen. Umm, you are okay with all of this, aren't you?"

I waved a dismissive hand. "You guys do what you need to do. Don't mind us."

Professor Houston nodded. "Thanks, Zack. Take it from me. I don't hear that nearly enough."

I watched the students take a load of wooden stakes into the cavity. Moments later, I heard repetitive whapping as the grid was strung out on the ground. Using a measuring tape, hammer, and a spool of red string, the entire floor was slowly transformed into a grid.

"You guys are thorough," I observed, as I leaned around the professor to stare at the dig site. "How is it you were available to come here on a single day's notice?"

"You caught me between digs," Steve explained. "I was about to request a meeting with my department head, to see about arranging my next excursion, when this was literally dropped in my lap."

"How many digs have you been on?" I asked. "Sherlock. Watson. Stop staring at the professor. It's getting creepy."

Both corgis were staring, unblinking, at Dr. Houston, as though he had just competed in a hot dog eating competition.

"They're just as friendly as I imagined," the professor confided. "Although, I'm not sure why they're staring at me so intently."

"That makes two of us," I admitted. "Do me a favor. Walk over there, would you? Now over there. Okay, you can come back. There's something about you they're absolutely loving. Did you sit on a plate of nachos or something?"

Dr. Houston snorted with laughter. "Wow, not that I'm aware of. To answer your question, I've been on fourteen digs, all across the world. Most, I will admit, have been here, in the United States."

"What was your most recent, if you don't mind me asking?"

"Well, I was in Luxor, Egypt, last month. I was

part of the team that helped excavate the new Lost Golden City. I don't suppose you've heard of it?"

"As a matter of fact, I think I have. How did you manage to get assigned that detail?"

"Hey, I'm just that good," Professor Houston deadpanned. He looked at me and broke out laughing. "I knew I couldn't say that and keep a straight face. Dr. Wolfe is that good. She's dropped some heavy research money into the expedition, so they reciprocated by allowing a couple of us to help out. Last year, I was in Turkey."

"Turkey, huh? Sure does sound like you get around."

"That one," Steve said, lowering his voice, "was a real eye-opener. I was in Karahan Tepe, excavating a site. What did I find? A whole lotta phallus-shaped pillars. Let me tell you, they never taught *that* in grad school."

"Dr. Houston?" Bobbi called.

The two of us turned to the large, jagged opening I had a hand in making in the foundation.

"Yes?"

"We're ready to begin digging the test pits. Do you want me and Noah to take one and you the other?"

"No, I think each of you has earned to the right to dig your own pit. You guys pick your own quadrant, but make sure it gives you enough room to move around. Speaking of which, how large are the quadrants?"

"The area isn't that big," Bobbi explained, "so we

laid out a grid with quadrants equaling two square meters."

"How many quadrants does that give us?" Professor Houston asked.

"Nine, with a tenth being about half the size."

"That'll do. Nice work. Get started, would you? I'll be right in."

My cell phone chose that time to ring. This time, since I'd added his number to my contacts, Burt's name popped up.

"Hey Burt, how's it …"

"Mr. Anderson!" Burt interrupted. "Please, I need you to come down to the shop. I am really sorry to say this, but my store has been robbed!"

"What? How in the …? Scratch that. I'll be right there."

I hung up the phone, looked at the Civil War cavity, as I was starting to call it, and then looked at the professor.

"You don't need me around here, do you?"

Professor Houston shook his head. "I shouldn't, no. Is everything okay?"

"That's what I need to go find out." I held out my phone. "Punch in your number for me, would you?"

Nodding, Steve took the phone and dialed his own cell. Once the professor's pocket was ringing, he hung up and handed my phone back.

"Thanks. I need to head out. You've got my number now, so if you guys need anything, just call, okay?"

"You got it, Zack. Leave this to us."

Gathering up the dogs--and for the record, neither wanted to budge--I started to walk away when, thinking better of it, pulled my phone back out and snapped a picture of the professor. Why Sherlock was fixated on the friendly archaeologist, I couldn't say. However, my corgis have been known to stare at some really strange things when working on a case. Why should this be any different?

Once the picture was taken, the dogs seemingly woke up, as if they were snapped out of a trance. They took one look at me, barked joyfully, and pulled me, like I was guiding a team of oxen pulling a plow, over to my Jeep. I didn't even have to pick Sherlock up. As soon as the door was open, he sailed by me, as though he had found a small trampoline and used it to get some extra lift. Watson, bless her heart, tried. She managed to get her front paws inside my car, but that was it. Thankfully, this wasn't the first time my little girl had tried to jump into my Jeep. I had outdoor tires on my personal vehicle, so it sat a little higher than most cars. There was no way she could've made it inside. Then again, I'm still impressed whenever Sherlock does it.

Giving my little girl a boost, the three of us hurried into town. Navigating my way through traffic, I drove past Cookbook Nook. Thinking ahead, and the simple fact I'm sure she would like to know, I gave Jillian a call and informed her what had happened, and where we were headed. She made me promise to keep her up to date.

As we approached Hidden Relics & Antiques, I could see a cop car parked out front. I also spotted Vance's Oldsmobile sedan parked nearby. Grabbing Sherlock and Watson's leashes, we headed into the store.

"Nothing like this has ever happened before," Burt was telling Vance. "I swore off violence the day I left the Rangers, but I'm telling you now, if I catch the punks who did this, then I'm gonna twist them into a pretzel. Ah, Mr. Anderson."

"Burt, are you okay? Hey, Vance. Fancy seeing you here."

"What a surprise, I know," my friend scoffed, without looking up from his tiny notebook. "You got here at what time this morning?"

"Around 6:30," Burt answered. "I came in through the back and immediately saw the mess."

"What did you do first?" Vance asked.

Burt leveled a gaze at my detective friend.

"Is that important?"

"Well, it's after 8 a.m. now," Vance pointed out. "You're telling me you waited over ninety minutes before letting us know you had a break-in?"

"I've never had a break-in before," Burt quietly mused. "It's my first ever. I was so shocked that I ended up doing a complete check on all my stock."

"Was anything missing?" Vance wanted to know.

"If there is, I haven't noticed it yet," Burt said.

JEFFREY POOLE

"Do you have any ideas who did it?" Vance continued.

Burt shook his head. "I don't know, but I have to wonder if it had something to do with Zack's chest."

The scratching of Vance's pen came to an immediate stop.

"Do you want to run that by me again?"

"Mr. Anderson left a Civil War trunk with me. He …"

"I know the one you're talking about," Vance interrupted. He turned to me with a look of incredulity on his face. "This trunk is from the foundation Tori told me about? It's from your old house?"

I nodded. "Yes, but I'm sure it doesn't have anything to do with Burt's store and the burglary attempt."

Vance leaned around Burt and pointed at the glass window next to the door. It had been shattered.

"Burglary attempt?" Vance repeated, shaking his head. "This wasn't any attempt, but a full-fledged break-in. Someone made it into this store and as Burt noted, made a mess of things. Was there any cash stolen?"

"No. I keep less than twenty in the cash register, and when I leave, I pop out the drawer, to let the perps know just how much you'd get if you chose to crack open the register."

"Other valuables?" Vance asked, returning his

attention to his notebook. "Pieces of jewelry? Silver, gold, and precious metals?"

"This is an antique store," Burt insisted. "I have a few pieces of jewelry here, collected from various estates, but nothing too expensive."

"All right," I sighed, "I'll ask it. What about the trunk? Was it in here when the place was searched?"

"It was," Burt confirmed.

Vance looked left, then right. "Where is it now? I don't see a trunk anywhere."

It was the first time I saw the big man smile today. A wide, cheeky grin appeared on Burt's rugged face.

"Those items were tucked away, safe and secure."

"You have a safe large enough to hold a foot locker?" I asked, as I turned to study the walls. I didn't see any paintings large enough to conceal a safe.

Burt nodded. He curled his index finger and motioned for us to follow him.

"I haven't shown anyone this before," the shop owner confessed. "I trust both of you to keep my secret. Will you do that for me? Forget about what you see here?"

The two of us nodded. Burt then headed toward the far back wall of his shop. Bemused, the four of us—two humans and two dogs—followed closely behind. Navigating around displays, wooden tables, and devices I didn't recognize, we were now looking at Burt's tiny office. Burt closed the office door, locked it, and then with me and Vance watching closely, he twisted the key in the lock a second time, only he reversed the direction, giving the knob a full half turn counter-clockwise. Then, he promptly stepped back.

"What are we doing?" Vance quietly asked.

Burt held a finger up to his lips. "Give it a moment. The system is old, and isn't often used."

"*What* isn't used that much?" I asked.

Movement in my peripheral vision caught my attention. Glancing down, I saw that both corgis were now head-tilting the floor in front of Burt's office. What happened next had me utterly convinced to find a way to install a secret door from the master bedroom to the game room in my new house.

A section of the tiled floor, a four-by-four grid of tile, if you want to get technical, which were comprised of eighteen inch by eighteen inch white tiles, suddenly sank an inch or two down, as if a giant had stepped on it and had activated a type of large button. Vance and I looked at each other as the floor rumbled for a few moments.

"Hop on," Burt instructed. He stooped to pick up the dogs, one under each arm. Both corgis turned to look at him with curiosity written all over their features. Shrugging, Vance and I took our places beside Burt just as the floor started *sinking*!

"It's an elevator!" Vance said, impressed.

Burt nodded. "That's right. No one knows this is

here, and I only go down there when I absolutely have to, and even then, it's only when the store is closed. This, gentlemen, is my storeroom. Mr. Anderson, if you look over there, then you'll see your trunk and the crates you brought in. They're perfectly fine, because I can't see how our burglar could even know this was down here."

"Do you really think someone was looking for this?" I asked, as Vance and I stepped over to the trunk. Burt set the dogs down and joined us. "If so, who would know that you even had it?"

"And that's the question I've been asking myself," Burt said. "You didn't tell anyone, did you?"

"Well, I did, but I don't think anyone I talked to would spread around the news."

"Who'd you tell?" Vance asked. His notebook was back in his hand.

"Well, you, for starters," I began. "Jillian obviously told Tori."

"Didn't you tell the university?" Vance asked.

I snapped my fingers. "That's right. Speaking of which, there's an archaeologist and several grad students excavating the site right now."

Vance turned to look at me. "Really? That was fast. Who'd you get? Does he have a bullwhip and a fedora?"

Burt grinned and looked away.

"Oh, ha ha. I wish. No, the person they sent over looks a lot like Lara Croft. You know, from Tomb Raider? Long, brown hair, guns on either hip, and

… man, close your mouth. I was just kidding! The University of Oregon sent over a professor by the name of Steve Houston. So, yeah, the university knows. Oh, and SOU knows, too."

"You called both institutions?" Burt asked.

"No, just SOU. They called the University of Oregon, since they obviously knew they didn't have an archaeology department. Oh, as long as we're naming names, the entire demolition crew knows about the find. Heck, they were the first in there."

Vance sighed. "So, you're telling me everybody knows about this by now. Got it. I don't think that helps us."

"So, what did you need me here for, Burt?" I asked, confused. "It doesn't look like anything was stolen."

"That's what I need to find out," Burt said. "I'm really sorry, but I should have catalogued everything you brought yesterday. As it is, I can't seem to remember if everything is here. Yes, I brought everything down here, as a precaution, and I've searched upstairs, but I need you to recall if anything is missing."

Shaking my head, I pointed at the dogs. "I'll do one better. Sherlock, Watson, is there something amiss with this place? Would you like to look around?"

Sherlock immediately pulled me over to the trunk, which was on the ground. Watson followed behind me, and then when we reached it, she joined her packmate. Together, they sniffed the trunk a few times. Sherlock then craned his neck to look at the hole in the ceiling, which now had a thin metal grating covering the opening, presumably for safety.

"Looks like they want to go back upstairs," Burt said. "Is your car out front? I can start loading your things up. You did mention the site is being excavated by an archaeological team, didn't you?"

"I did, and that's a good idea. Thanks, Burt."

I handed him my keys as I scooped up Watson, and Vance did the same for Sherlock. Once we were back at ground level, us clueless bipeds followed my dogs around the store as Sherlock and Watson decided to sniff *everything*. And, much to my surprise, we stopped not once, nor twice, but three times.

The first was at a glass display with a highly decorated metal plate inside. I could see all manner of decorations hammered onto its surface, which included an ancient sun symbol, rays spreading out from the sun, and then some crude animals.

"That's a gaudy looking thing, isn't it?" Vance quietly murmured, as he came up behind me to see what I was looking at.

"Tell me about it. I don't know why the dogs selected it but I'm gonna take a picture. If it's pertinent, then they'll move on."

"They're moving on," Vance reported, after I snapped a few pictures.

Next, the dogs then stopped at a large display of old west artifacts. This counter-high glass display held handcuffs, revolvers, an old Winchester rifle, a sheriff's badge, and a few photos of what looked like a jail. Once again, the dogs wouldn't budge until I snapped a few photos.

"Plate and the Old West," Vance mused, as we followed the dogs. "Are you taking notes?"

"It's all on my phone," I said, shrugging. "It won't make any sense until we go through them."

"And even then, it might not," Vance joked.

"True. Now what? Sherlock, Watson, what are we looking at?"

"What *are* we looking at?" Vance inquired, puzzled.

We were standing before a bookcase.

"Books? Seriously? Do you guys see how many there are? I don't suppose you could narrow it down for us?"

I heard a snort of exasperation from Sherlock. He nudged the bookcase with his nose and then turned to look up at me, as though I was the dunderhead for not figuring it out. Confused, I looked at Vance, who shrugged.

"Don't look at me, pal. They're your dogs."

"Fine. See? I'm taking a picture of the books."

Vance stepped forward so he could read some of the titles.

"Anything good?" I asked.

"Not that I can see."

"There are plenty of good reads in there," Burt

contradicted, from behind me. "They're historical tomes, and they're all about Oregon state history in some fashion."

"Huh. I did not know that."

Burt handed me my keys. "It was a tight fit, but you're all loaded up. Have your dogs looked at anything besides these books?"

"We stopped by that display with the one plate inside. Then, they stopped at the cabinet with all the western memorabilia in it. You know, the one with the handcuffs and the guns. Tell me something. Those handcuffs--are they the real deal?"

"That set is from the turn of the century, and it also includes leg shackles. Interested?"

"I have to admit, I'm very tempted," I told the big man.

"They're yours, in exchange for everything you've done for me."

"Burt, I didn't do that to get some free stuff. You're a businessman. You need to be paid for your merchandise, so you ..."

"... won't take no for an answer," Burt finished. He walked back to the display, pulled out the cuffs and the leg restraints, and headed to the counter. After they were carefully packaged and wrapped, he handed them to me. "It makes me feel better that I can offer you something in exchange. You're not going to take that away from me, are you?"

I had to laugh. "Have you been talking to Jillian?"

Burt grinned and shoved his hands into his pockets.

"Remember, when you're ready to sell that trunk, and anything else you found with it, I'm ready to buy."

"You're on, pal."

Vance and I walked the dogs outside. Once Sherlock and Watson were loaded in my Jeep, I was about to say goodbye to Vance when my phone rang, for what felt like the umpteenth time that day.

"Hello?"

"Mr. Anderson? It's Professor Houston."

"Hey, Steve. What's up?"

"Umm, have you got a minute?"

That one question caused the hairs on the back of my neck to stand straight up.

"You definitely have my attention now. What is it? Did you find the remains of Private Howell?"

"Private Howell? You know his name? How?"

"I'll tell you about it when I see you. I'm just leaving the antique store. I've got all the stuff with me."

"Good. We all want to take a look. But, that's not why I'm calling. You wanted to know if we found Private Howell's remains? Well, I'm pretty sure he's one of them."

"One of them?" I repeated, as I shared a brief look with Vance. I placed the call on speakerphone so he could hear it, too.

"Yes, one of them. Our test pits have uncovered

at least four different individuals, Zack."

FOUR

Two days later, my thoughts were hopelessly lost on the British Isles, exploring villages, visiting popular tourist destinations, and staying at small, cozy inns, complete with hearths in every room. Having my hero win an all-expense paid trip to Cymru which, if you didn't know, was in Wales, I was busy researching sights to see, activities to do, and what type of food I'd expect him to find. Lemonade would look like clear water, clotted cream would quickly become a favorite, and stopping for a toasty would become the highlight of the day.

All right, with the protagonist in town, I could have him hop on the nearest tour bus and take a quick tour, but ... no, that wouldn't work. He was supposed to have some interactions with a few other characters on that bus, and he hasn't met them yet. In fact, he won't meet that particular person until he's in the gift shop located around the corner from the castle, so that part was going to get deleted. At this rate, my main character would reach the castle way too soon. I had to slow him down, which meant I had to come up with something I called *filler material*, that is, something that would happen, or be discussed, which further develops the character's personality. Many times, I'll include a piece of humor if the situation is getting too dark, or possibly throw in a phone call, which will enrich the story, but also slow it down a smidge.

Once at the castle, I'll have him join a tour group, so that he can wander around the majestic Conwy Castle without arousing suspicion. But, how would I get him inside the northwest tower in time for his accidental encounter with the lovely Ms. Isabeau Cambrioleur? And why would she be in that tower, too? There had to be a reason. Meeting with an accomplice? Picking up something that had been surreptitiously dropped off?

Let me stop right here for a moment and pose a question. Have you ever wondered what goes on inside an author's head? Granted, I can't speak for all of them, but as for this one, well, this is pretty much the way I write. I have an idea what I'd like to write about, but I have to make it believable. I think most people would be surprised to learn that practically all authors aren't always pecking away at their keyboards. Nuh-uh. Most will be leaning back in their chairs, wondering how they're going to pull off a particular scene. And the others— they'll be the ones researching scenarios online to verify whether or not it's feasible and to make sure the facts are straight, because the last thing we want is to be called out on an online review.

That's why so many authors try so hard to stay in the *zone*, meaning for once, the words are flowing freely, the ideas are legitimate, and—sadly—most times, your fingers simply can't keep up.

That's what I was presently *not* doing: enjoying time in my own zone. No matter how hard I tried, every time I started writing, a problem would present itself, and I had to make darn certain I wasn't writing myself into a corner. It's hard to get into the zone, let alone stay in it, when you're constantly tearing apart your own ideas.

Leaning back in my chair, arms crossed, I contemplated what I could make my female character do. An idea formed, and a smile appeared on my face, when I was forcefully brought back to the present.

"*Woof.*"

"Oh, you gotta be kidding me," I groaned, as I sat forward and pushed my laptop away from me. Waiting a few moments confirmed that it was, of course, Sherlock. Then, I heard him woof again. "All right, all right, I'm coming."

Walking down the hall and into the main living room, I found both dogs exactly where they were on the previous day: stretched out on the couch, watching television. Sherlock, however, was ignoring me and staring at the television screen, transfixed. Walking around the couch so that I was standing behind the sofa with the dogs, I saw that yet another pizza commercial was playing on the screen.

Casting a sideways glance at Sherlock, and then down at Watson, who was only interested in belly scratches, I pulled out my phone and snapped a few pictures. What was the deal with pizza, anyway? Did Sherlock know where we were planning on *not* going in a few days? It shouldn't make any difference to him. It's not like I have ever shared any of it with him. Yes, I will give my dogs a few tidbits of people food if I know it's safe for canine consumption. However, with regards to pizza, I typically will have some variation of pork as a topping, and that, I knew, was bad for dogs. Plus, I've had Harry tell me on more than one occasion that I really should lay off the dinner scraps.

In my defense, they weren't scraps. They were little pieces of real food: piece of banana, cheese, strawberry, or anything else I knew the corgis liked. Oh, they didn't get much of it, so no hate mail, thank you very much. Just a little piece to let them know Dad is willing to share what he has with them.

But, back to the television. Why would Sherlock and Watson want me to look at a pizza commercial? If memory serves, and trust me, lately, it *hasn't*, the last time Sherlock woofed at the TV, I do recall there being a pizza commercial on, too. How it related to the Civil War was anyone's guess. I held up my camera.

"There, see, I took a few pictures. Will there be anything else, your Royal Canineships?"

Sherlock snorted once and returned his attention to the show. This time, the program being shown was a documentary-style video following a family of squirrels. Neither dog made a peep, and neither of them moved a muscle. I don't even think they blinked. However, it looked like the program was just wrapping up, because the credits were now flashing on the screen, and both dogs were rousing themselves, as if waking from a trance.

Sherlock looked expectantly at me and wiggled his rear. Watson wove her way between my legs. Was it me, or did they want something?

"You're buttering me up," I told the two dogs. "Out with it. What do you guys want?"

Sherlock yipped once, jumped down from the couch, and ran into the kitchen, with Watson close on his heels. By the time I made it inside Carnation Cottage's kitchen, both dogs had placed themselves before a very specific cupboard and were sitting primly, as if awaiting inspection.

"You want a Kong, is that it?"

Those hollow rubber toys, designed to be stuffed with all of the corgis' favorite treats, were the next best thing to television shows created especially for pets. Most of the times, each dog could work his or her way through their Kong in about forty-five minutes. If I smeared the inside with a tablespoon of creamy peanut butter, then at least an hour, maybe an hour and a half.

Once the dogs were once again preoccupied, I returned to my desk, intent on picking up where I left off. Just like before, it wasn't meant to be. My overactive imagination kicked in and started thinking about everything Professor Houston and his students had found thus far. When he called me to let me know they had tentatively identified four different skeletons, it turned out that it wasn't necessarily accurate. There weren't four skeletons, but *six*. Half a dozen Union cavalry soldiers, more than likely from the great state of Oregon, had lost their lives in that little section of my land. Why? Better yet, how? Why hadn't they been given a proper burial?

Compounding matters was that the bodies weren't discovered in a mass grave, but in their own separate burial sites.

"There's definitely something wrong here," I grumbled to myself, as I systematically began closing my files, so I could shut down my computer.

I had reached a point in my life where I knew what I was going to do, how I was going to behave, and therefore, what I *should* be doing about it. As much as I'd like to, I wasn't going to be able to return to Wales. That was a passing moment, and it was most assuredly over. Since I wasn't going to think about my book, then that meant I could free up some time to start thinking about this case.

I had also asked, since I'm sure you've wondered by now, whether or not it was apparent something bad had befallen those men. Did the bones show any sign of trauma? I remember asking the professor that which had been on my mind and I fervently hoped the answer was a solid no: did the bones show any type of scoring, or ... *gnawing*? Professor Houston had assured me there were no signs of foul play. However, he was just as confused as I was as to why the remains of six individuals were in that hidden cavity.

My cell announced an incoming call, causing me to flinch in my seat.

"Zack? It's Professor Houston."

"Oh, Lord. Do I even want to know what you guys found this time?"

"No, it's nothing like that. We have a request."

Taken aback, I paused longer than I should.

"Zack? Still there?"

"Yeah, sorry. What do you guys need?"

"If possible, I need you to try and keep this area clear."

"Huh? What, did one of my cars move on their own?"

The professor laughed. "No, what I mean is, the local press has learned about the discovery of the bodies here, and ..."

"Wait," I interrupted, frowning. "How could the press have done that? It's not like your discovery has been broadcast over the police scanner. My wife and I haven't breathed a word. That would leave …"

"I've already given him a stern lecture of the importance of not bragging about what we find during our excavations, especially when frequenting a bar."

I groaned aloud. "One of your students. Oh, that's just great. News vans are there now, is that it?"

"One is here, setting up, and a quick search online shows that, more than likely, more are on the way."

"Well, I know from experience that they can't stay there if I don't give permission. That means I'll … wait. Let's try this. Go up to the reporter and hand him your phone."

"It's a lady," Professor Houston contradicted. "And, I'm on my way."

"What does she look like?" I asked.

"Do you know that many?" Steve asked, stifling a laugh.

"It just goes to show you how many times I've been the focus of a whole lot of unwanted attention."

"All right, I'm approaching the news van. They see me coming and they're preparing their camera. The lady reporter has blond hair, looks to be older than me but younger than you …"

"Thanks a lot, pal," I grumbled, when the professor took a breath.

"… and is wearing a bright yellow two-piece suit."

"Professional attire?" I asked.

"Sure looks that way," Steve confirmed.

As I explained to the professor earlier, I have had encounters with more than my fair share of reporters during my time in PV. Only a select few were pleasant enough, and left when I told them to. The others had to be escorted off my property, so I was really hoping it wouldn't have to come to that. Then again, the one reporter I knew who was a stickler for ignoring requests to vacate the premises was a lady by the name of Clara Springfield.

"Good afternoon," I heard a female voice begin. "Clara Springfield, Channel 11 News. You're not Mr. Zachary Anderson, are you?"

"I am not," the professor explained.

"Cut feed," I heard the reporter say, letting out an irritated sigh.

"But," Steve continued, "I have him on the phone right here. Would you be willing to talk to him?"

"Clara Springfield, Channel 11 News," the reporter informed me, the moment she got on the line. "Is this Mr. Zachary Anderson?"

"It is, and you can drop the formalities," I told the reporter. "We've met before. I ordered you off my property when you thought I was guilty of murder. I do believe we've met a few other times, too, but that one stands out the most. Remember me now?"

"Oh. Uh, I do, yes."

Was it me, or did the voice sound deflated?

"Look, I have a proposition for you."

"Oh? What do you want, Mr. Anderson?"

"Leave now, and let my workers continue to do their thing. In exchange, I'll give you an exclusive interview when all of this is over and done with. Do we have a deal?"

"You'll willingly give me an interview?"

"Once everything is said and done," I reminded her. "There's a lot to do first, but when it is, I'll let you know. Unfortunately, I just don't have a date and time for you."

"How do I know you won't forget our arrangement?" the reporter suspiciously asked. "How do I know you're not saying this just to get me to leave?"

"You're leaving whether you like it or not," I told the reporter. "Willing or not. But, I'd rather not make a scene. I'm clearly not there. Instead of having you brought up on trespassing charges, I thought we could come to a more amicable arrangement. Leave now, and when I'm done with everything, I'll invite you and your team out to the winery and tell you all about what happened."

"You're not making this deal with anyone else, are you?"

"Only if you refuse and make me head back out there," I said. "Otherwise, I'll have you escorted off and will reach out to another station. This offer is going once …"

In the background, I heard a male voice say she should take the deal.

"Going twice …

"All right, all right, we accept the deal."

"Fantastic. Ms. Springfield, leave a business card with the owner of the phone, and I'll reach out once I'm ready. And thanks."

"That was impressive," the professor told me, once he was back on the phone. "Now you have to give an exclusive interview?"

"Whatever. It's a small price to pay. Now, tell me, how goes the search there? Find anything worth sharing?"

"Well, I can start describing body parts," Professor Houston said. I could picture him grinning. "But, in the past, whenever I do that, it tends to make people sick, so I'm trying to get into a habit of asking first."

Sitting at my desk at Carnation Cottage with my phone set to speakerphone, I held up my hands in a time-out manner, not realizing the archaeologist couldn't see me.

"Thanks for asking. The answer is absolutely not, so if there's nothing else, I think I'm good. But, if you need anything from me, just ask."

"Will do, Mr. Anderson. Thanks."

I spent the next thirty minutes trying futilely to get the story flowing again, but it just wasn't meant to be. My Welsh story would have to wait until inspiration struck. Or, more likely, construction had begun on my new house.

And *that* was all it took to get me thinking about those poor souls who had just been recovered back at Lentari Cellars. Burt had been able to identify the unit. Quite frankly, he had been incredibly helpful as of late, so perhaps it was time to thank our friendly, neighborhood giant for his help? I seem to recall Burt enjoyed wine. A bottle from Lentari Cellars didn't seem like much of a price to pay.

Pulling out my cell, I sent a quick text message off to Jillian.

> DOES BURT LIKE WINE? GOING TO THANK HIM WITH A BOTTLE FROM LC

> GEWÜRZTRAMINER

> THANK YOU!

> THERE'S A BOTTLE IN MY CUPBOARD. YOU CAN HAVE IT IF YOU REPLACE IT

> I WILL. THX!

Well, *that* made it easy. Retrieving the long-necked bottle from Jillian's kitchen, I gathered up the dogs and headed for my Jeep. The weather outside was a very pleasant seventy-two degrees. Giving the dogs a rare treat, I decided to remove my Jeep's hardtop and get some much needed fresh air. But, it also meant clipping the dogs into the seat belts, the only time I'll do so.

The drive was uneventful; the dogs refrained from woofing at anything, and I was actually looking forward to talking about antiques with the former Ranger. Parking outside his shop, the dogs and I headed inside with the bottle of wine tucked inside my jacket.

"Mr. Anderson!" Burt exclaimed, delighted. "Oh, I hope you're going to tell me about something else you and your team found."

"I'm not actually," I confessed. "Not this time. I mean, if we do, you're the first person I'm talking to, but, as for this time, I think we're good. In fact, here. I have something for you. It's a bottle of Gewürztraminer, courtesy of Lentari Cellars. A little birdie told me you are a fan. Think of it as a thanks for everything you've done so far."

Two huge, thick arms were crossed over their owner's chest.

"You're doing *me* all these favors, and you're thanking *me*?"

"You know what I mean," I said. "All the help in identifying the stuff I brought in. All the help in figuring out which company these men belonged to." I held out the bottle. "I'm told Lentari Cellars makes a mean bottle of wine, you know."

Smiling, and giving a slight shake of his head, Burt held out an enormous hand. The bottle looked fake in comparison to the fingers that wrapped around it.

"I think I should have brought a second bottle," I chuckled.

Burt waved off my comment.

"Have you done any more research about the 4th?" he asked me.

"I have, yeah," I admitted.

"And?"

"And I haven't found a darn thing. There is literally no mention of this unit anywhere in the Civil War history books."

Burt pulled out his cell, tapped the screen a few times, and then set the phone on the counter.

"You just haven't talked to the right people."

We heard a faint ringing on the phone. Burt had dialed someone, and now we were waiting for whoever it was to answer the call.

"Thank you for calling the National Archives Building. How may I direct your call?"

Burt leaned over the phone.

"Media desk, please. Department of Military and Civil Records, thank you."

"One moment, please," the receptionist instructed.

"Is your contact even working today?" I whispered.

"She's there, Monday through Friday, so unless she's working on something else, she'll be at her desk."

The elevator music on Burt's phone was suddenly replaced by ringing.

"Department of Military and Civil Records," a female voice said. "How can I help you?"

"Angie? It's Burt Johnson, PV."

"Burt! You big stud! Calling me twice in one week. What can I do for you?"

"Well, I have someone here who could use your help as well, and now he's currently laughing at me, so thanks for that."

Burt might have sounded embarrassed, but I could tell he really wasn't. After a comment like that, I'm sure I'd be beet red by now.

"You bet, hot stuff. What do you need? Who's there?"

"This is Zack Anderson," I announced, when Burt looked over at me. "I'm the owner of the property where all these Civil War items were found. I was hoping I could get you to use some of your magic for me, too."

"I'll do my best, sweetness."

"Angelica, meet Zack," Burt said. "Zack, this is Angelica Adler, foremost expert on the Civil War and the records this country has from that period of time."

"Pleased to meet you, sugar," Angelica crooned. "You can call me Angie, too. So, hit me with your best shot. You want to know about the 4th Oregon Volunteer Infantry Regiment?"

"Well, how long would it take for you to pull all that data back up?" I asked.

"Let's see, click once, click twice, and there it is. I bookmarked it last time," Angelica explained. "I will say there's not too much available about this unit. I'd have to go through the files to be certain."

"What do you have about them?" I asked. "What can you tell me about that unit?"

"Everyone enlisted in Portland," Angelica said, her voice adopting a neutral tone as she spoke, suggesting she was reading a printout. She cleared her throat and her voice returned to normal.

"Oregon didn't play too much of a role in the Civil War."

"Understandable," I said, nodding.

"The only thing soldiers serving in Oregon were responsible for were guarding travel routes and Indian reservations," Angelica continued. "They were also known to escort emigrant wagon trains and were also tasked with protecting settlers from Indian attacks."

I looked at Burt, amazed. "Indian attacks? In Oregon? I don't think I've ever seen that in a history book before."

"What else do you have?" Burt asked.

"Roads."

Burt and I shared a look.

"Roads?" he asked. "What about them?"

"When there wasn't much to do, many soldiers pitched in and built roads," Angelica explained, in her neutral voice. "Ongoing skirmishes with prospectors and Indians regarding newfound gold fields in Oregon and Idaho also took up a significant part of their time."

"I forgot about the Oregon state gold rush," I admitted.

"You of all people should be well versed in its history," Burt said, giving me a nudge on the shoulder.

"Why?" Angelica wanted to know.

"Just an inside joke for anyone here in town," Burt said, with a gleam in his eye.

"That's old news," I joked. I *might* have helped

look for a lost gold mine a little while ago. "What else do you have for me?"

"That's about it, I'm afraid," Angelica reluctantly admitted. "I don't have a list of names for you; the image is too badly smudged to have any idea what it says. But, what I *can* tell you is that there are many hundreds of thousands of records pertaining to the Civil War. Some have been digitized, which is what I have access to, but it means that most have not. I'd have to dust off the microfilm boxes to know for sure."

"Microfilm? Seriously?"

"There are boxes and boxes of it, sugar," Angelica told me. "The unit you're talking about will undoubtedly be in there. It's just a matter of finding it."

"And, er, is this something you're willing to do?" I asked, uncertain I wanted to know the answer.

"Well, what's it worth to ya, honey?" Angelica not-so-delicately asked.

"What do you want?" I countered. "There must be something that you're interested in."

"Well, now that you put it like that, I guess I could say yes, there is something I want."

I looked over at Burt, who refused to meet my eyes.

"I'm not going to like this, am I?"

The antiques dealer kept his face parked in neutral and shrugged.

"First, I have a question for you, Burt."

My friend nodded. "Go ahead, Angie."

"Is this the guy you were telling me about? The one who happens to be an author?"

"Yes."

"A romance author?"

"Yes."

"Is he the author of the *Derelict Moors* saga?"

Burt shook his head and wouldn't meet my eyes.

"Yes."

"You've talked about me?" I whispered, to which I was ignored.

"I've never met an author before," Angelica said. Right about then, I noticed the eagerness in her voice. "So, I have a proposition for you. If you name a character after me, then I'll gladly do this favor for you."

If I had a dollar for every time I heard those words, then I'd be a rich man.

"Angelica, that's something I don't do," I said, after a couple moments had passed. It wasn't necessarily true. I mean, I *did* just that for my friend Vance's wife, Tori, but that was an extenuating circumstance. "What I *would* be willing to do is have you join my team of betas."

"What does that mean?" Angelica asked.

"My betas are a group of people who read the books before they're published. They are friends and family of mine who want to help me polish the story by offering their input. For example, my betas will not only look for typos—I have several editors who will do that—but also for continuity errors, plot holes, and so on. They've been with me for years, and know my writing style inside and out."

"You're inviting me to join this team?" Angie asked, surprised.

"In exchange for some information, yeah," I said. "Anything you can tell me about this particular unit would be incredibly helpful."

Close to a full minute passed. I looked at Burt, wondering what was taking so long. He held a finger to his lips and indicated I should wait. Finally, Angelica came back on the line.

"Very well, you have a deal! Oh, this is so exciting! I can say I helped write a book!"

"Well, you ... yes, you would," I finally admitted, dropping my objection. She could think whatever she wanted, I suppose. "Thank you, Angelica. Give Burt all your contact details. I'll forward them to my publisher, okay?"

"You got it, Mr. Anderson."

Once the call had ended, Burt let out a breath.

"I am very sorry about that. I had no idea she was going to weasel a favor out of you."

"It's okay. Like I told her, I can't do the character thing, but I can add her to my beta readers team. Most people get a kick out of it."

"That's quick thinking," Burt decided.

"Do you think she'll be able to find anything on microfilm?"

"If anyone can do it, then she's the one who can," Burt confirmed. "Again, I am so sorry she put you on the spot like that. I can tell you that I'm not too pleased with how she handled that situation."

"Don't worry about it," I said, hoping to just brush off the concern. Then, inspiration struck. "But, there is something you can do for me."

Burt perked up. "Oh? Name it."

"Admit you were on some of those World's Ultimate Strongman competitions."

Burt actually burst out laughing.

"This again?"

"I swear, man," I continued, "I've seen you on it before. For my own peace of mind, were you?"

Burt was silent as he studied me. After a few moments, much to my amazement, he started nodding.

"Fine. You win. Yes, I was."

"Holy crap on a cracker! I knew it!"

"You're the only one who wouldn't let it go," Burt chuckled.

"Did … did you win?"

Burt held up two fingers. "Twice. 1989 and 1991."

I grinned at the huge man and nodded. "That's so cool. Thanks for finally telling me."

"For all you've done for me, and my business, it was the least I could do."

I roused Sherlock and Watson from their nap and was about to head for the door when I turned back to the big man, who was returning to his place behind the counter.

"One final question, Burt."

"Go ahead."

"You competed for the United States, didn't you? I wonder why I never noticed your name."

Burt shook his head.

"I never competed for this country. I competed for my own."

I had just pushed his door open when I turned. So did the dogs, too, as though they were just as curious as I was.

"Oh? Which country?"

"My name doesn't give it away?" Burt asked, as he leaned against the counter. "Add an *a* in the middle of it and you should have your answer."

I'm sure my face was a picture of confusion.

"Burat?"

Sherlock snorted.

"Well, that's a new one on me. I was talking about my last name."

"Johnson. Oh, I get it. Johanson?"

"You got it, Mr. Anderson."

"Why'd you change your name?"

"It was easier, and all my siblings changed their names when they came over, too. In Sweden, children will typically take their father's first name and add *son* to the end of it. As you may have guessed, my father's name was Johan. Hence, Johanson. Here, in the United States, some of my brothers went with Johanson, while others went with Johnson. One even went with our mother's maiden name. There's no set naming system in place."

"You learn something new every day. Thanks,

Burt. Keep me posted if Angelica finds anything."

"I will, Mr. Anderson."

FIVE

T he following day, after receiving yet another piece of celebrity fan mail, forwarded by my publisher, asking whether or not I was planning on writing a sequel to *Heart of Èire*, I decided to get Vance's take on it. After all, the only reason I wrote that particular book in the first place was as a favor to him. Maybe I should explain.

Vance wanted to do something nice for his and Tori's fifteenth wedding anniversary, so he approached me and asked if there was any way I could use Tori as the basis of one of my characters. Well, I did one better and proposed to write a book that featured her as the main protagonist. Fiction, of course. Long story short, that book earned me a spot on the coveted *New York Times* Best Seller's list for the first time ever. Set during the great Potato Famine in Ireland, Tori's character faced insurmountable odds to keep her family safe and fed. While I can say I enjoyed writing *Heart of Èire*, I had planned on it being a stand-alone title.

However, when you receive personalized messages from your favorite celebrities, asking when the sequel is going to be released, I figured it might be worth another look. The caveat to that would be to develop a story worthy as a sequel. It had to be feasible, believable, and more importantly, tie in with the first.

Therefore, I was going to have to give it some serious thought. Before I did that, though, I wanted my friend's opinion about it. After all, since he was the one who started this whole idea, I've been splitting the royalties with him, fifty-fifty. Did I have to? No. Nowhere was it written that I had to share the profits of something *I* wrote. However, *they* are the reason it was written in the first place. So, we share in the proceeds. Seeing how the monthly royalty checks were in the mid five figures, with one month actually hitting six, neither of us were in a position to complain.

As I pulled into the police station's parking lot, and chose a spot, I noticed that, for once, the number of open parking spaces was considerable. Was the PVPD having a slow day?

Exiting, and lifting the dogs down to the ground, I also noticed both Sherlock and Watson had perked up. Both pairs of ears were sticking straight up. Sherlock then decided he didn't want to move, and promptly sat.

"What are you doing? Come on. We've been here before. Lord knows, we have. I can't even begin to think of how many times we've walked through those doors, so this shouldn't be a surprise. Sherlock? Why aren't you moving, pal? Watson? Come on. Try to get him to move, would you?"

Both dogs settled to the sidewalk that ran in front of the station.

"What are you doing? Come on guys, I don't get it. You only do this if … wait. Is this what you want?" I had pulled my cell out of my pocket and held it down for the two corgis to see. "You want me to take a picture of this place? What in the world for? You know what, fine, you win. Look, I'm taking a picture. I took two. Happy?"

They were. Both returned to their feet and pulled on their leashes, as though *I* was the one holding us up. Dogs.

"Hi, Zack!" a woman's cheerful voice said.

Looking up, I saw that Julie Watt, who happened to be married to my best friend here in town, was manning the information counter. While not a police officer, Julie helped out wherever she was needed, whether it was as a dispatcher on the radio, or fielding requests at the front desk.

"Is everything all right? What are you doing here? Oh, look! It's Sherlock and Watson. Hello, you adorable dogs. How are you today? Look what I have for you!"

A small clear baggie was produced. Inside were little bits of cooked dough, the same used in making bagels. Bagel Bites, made by Taylor Adams, of Farm House Bakery, were a staple to every business in Pomme Valley. Why? Well, I'm certain it was because PV is a very pet-friendly town. Unless the business was a restaurant with no outdoor terraces, most stores welcomed our furry friends with open arms. The police station, it would seem, was no different.

Sherlock and Watson sprinted for the small doorway which led to the other side of the main police counter. I had to drop both leashes, lest the corgis clothesline themselves with their mad dash to see who could get to the treat quickest. By the time I made it around the counter, Sherlock and Watson were both stretched out by Julie's feet, crunching away on their treats, and flat-out ignoring me. Seriously, I could be held up at gunpoint and I don't think either of the dogs would have cared.

"Are your Royal Canineships ready now?" I asked, throwing a healthy bit of sarcasm into my voice.

The dogs continued to ignore me. They finished their goodies, stood, gave themselves a good shake, and then—and only then—looked up at me.

"Did you forget I was here? Boogers. Don't mind us, Julie. We're on our way to see Vance. I saw his car outside. He's not working on a case, is he?"

"Not that I'm aware of," Julie admitted, slipping off the headset she had been wearing. "As a matter of fact, it's kinda slow today. It's probably the slowest I've seen in a while. Then again, you're here, so that ought to pick things up a bit."

"Hardy har har. You've been talking to Vance

again, haven't you?"

Julie laughed and made to swat my arm, only the phone started to ring. Slipping the headset back on, I left her to take the call.

"Sherlock, Watson, let's go. We're off to find Vance."

I found my detective friend in his office, trying valiantly to type out some report on his computer. The glasses he hated wearing were perched precariously on the end of his nose, his back was as straight as a board, and the two index fingers he was using to type looked sore. In the time it took for us to walk into his small office, I heard him sigh no less than five times.

"Someone doesn't seem to be having a good day."

Vance looked up, saw that it was me, and whipped off his glasses, as though he had been caught doing something illegal. I don't know what he was worried about, since I know full well his eyes are bad enough to warrant some extra help. However, I also know he was embarrassed to use them, so I was trying to go out of my way to not make him feel uncomfortable.

"Did I catch you at a bad time?"

"God, no," Vance said, as he pushed away from his computer. "If you tell me you need help working that Civil War case of yours, then you will have made my year."

"Sorry, pal," I said, pulling out a chair in front of his desk. "I still have that archaeologist and his students excavating the encampment, so they've got it under control."

"Figures," Vance said, sighing. "What brings you here?"

"I've got something to run by you."

"Sure. Fire away."

I sat back in the chair and studied my friend.

"I've been asked, for what feels like the umpteenth time, whether or not I'm planning on writing a sequel to *Heart of Èire*."

Intrigued, Vance leaned forward to rest his elbows on his desk.

"Oh? Whatcha tell them?"

"That it was written as a stand-alone story, and that no plans were in the works."

Satisfied, Vance nodded. He started to lean back in his chair when he caught sight of my face.

"You're grinning. What are you smiling for?" Vance wanted to know. "Is there something you're not telling me?"

"You could say that."

"I *did* say that. What's going on?"

"Well, I've told you about some of the celebrities who have reached out, haven't I?"

"You have. Vicki and Tiffany are thrilled to death every time they hear about a new one who has written. So, who was it this time?"

Vicki and Tiffany are the names of Vance's two daughters, in case you didn't know.

"This time? How do you feel about Rosie Huntington-Whitely?"

Vance cocked his head.

"Who?"

"You don't know who that is?"

"Should I? Wait a moment. Isn't that …?"

"Jason Statham's fiancée, yes it is."

"Jason Statham! And his wife …"

"Fiancée," I corrected.

"… fiancée," Vance amended, "asked about our book?"

I grinned at Vance, who immediately blushed.

"Sorry. I meant *your* book. You know what I mean."

"Yeah, I do, and don't sweat it. Apparently, *Heart of Èire* is his fiancée's favorite book, and she would love to see another story with all the same characters. So, here's my question to you. How would you feel about trying to come up with a plot for a sequel?"

"Jason Statham. Holy cow."

"Are you okay?"

"Yeah, yeah, sure. Umm … what were we talking about?"

"You're fan-girling over a movie star, aren't you?"

"He's my favorite actor," Vance finally admitted.

"I figured he was. It's why I brought it up. Anyway, want to help me come up with something?"

"Come up with something?" Vance repeated, confused. "Are you talking about a plot? Come on, how hard could that be?"

"For us, it's going to be challenging," I admitted. "I wrote *Heart of Éire* as a single story. Do you know what that means?"

Vance shook his head. "No, sorry."

"It means that there are no loose ends. No plot holes, no unresolved issues. If a sequel is going to be written, then we need to come up with an objective that's feasible, believable, and bankable."

"Bankable," Vance chuckled, shaking his head. "Zack, I feel like I have no say in this whatsoever. After all, you were kind enough to split the proceeds from the book with us. And, for the record, I had no idea so much money could be made."

"People love to read," I said, offering my friend a smile. "And, once word gets out that there's a *can't-put-it-down* book out there everyone is raving about, then it's bound to make a penny or two. Think about it. In this day and age, everybody has a device that allows you to store thousands of books. Even audiobooks."

"You're talking about our phones, right?" Vance asked.

I laughed. "Yes, I am. But, there are still die-hards out there who enjoy picking up the real thing and reading the old-fashioned way."

Vance held up a hand. "I'd be one of them."

"I'd rather read on my tablet," I admitted. "But, I still have quite a few paperbacks and hardcovers at my house. Had. Past tense. The new house—It's going to have a two-story library, and a secret reading room for Jillian, only she doesn't know, so keep that to ourselves."

"You're the last true romantic, pal," Vance observed, giving me a grin. "All right, if you're game, and if we can come up with something for Tori's character to do, then I say we go for it. You, however, have the final say, 'cause you're the one doing all the work."

I shrugged. "I enjoy it, so I don't really view it as work. What do you say we discuss it with the ladies this Friday?"

"Sounds like a plan. Where did you want to go again?"

"And I thought my memory was bad. You've already forgotten, haven't you? Wait. We were going to try to find something besides pizza, weren't we?"

Vance looked pensive for a few moments before nodding.

"That's right. I had forgotten, and for once, I'll admit it. My stomach has been bothering me today, so I'm glad we're looking for other options. Want me to pick one?"

"Sure, I'd be willing to entertain a few ideas. My only request is that you don't pick the Chateau. I don't think *my* stomach can take it."

Sherlock woofed just then, which made me smile. I thought the feisty corgi believed I was making plans without him, and for the record, he was right this time. However, the little booger was looking straight at me, as though he was warning me to play nice.

"Judas," I accused, giving my tri-colored boy a good scratching. "Watson, you still love me, don't you?"

Watson immediately rolled onto her back and gazed up at me with adoring eyes.

"That's more like it."

Sherlock snorted once and lost interest.

The Chateau I mentioned just so happened to be Jillian's favorite restaurant. It might have something to do with it being the fanciest. Formal attire wasn't required, but highly recommended. Restaurant patrons typically wore semi-formal attire, which meant—as a guy—you should be wearing nice pants with a collared shirt and tie. For the record, it wasn't my first choice of apparel. Thankfully, my detective friend was shaking his head, which indicated he had someplace else in mind.

"How about Tre Formaggio?"

"Italian? Hmm. What about Marauder's Grill?"

"Too much cholesterol," Vance said. He noted my incredulous look and sighed. "I had a checkup a while back. My labs came back and promptly told me my good cholesterol was low, and the bad was high. I didn't even know there was such a thing as *good* cholesterol. I mean, it was low, so I figured I was in the clear. Nope. Bad cholesterol was much higher than it should be, so now I have to watch what I eat until it gets under control."

"All right, I'll give you that one. Hey, how about

Casa de Joe's?"

The restaurant name sounded unusual, but Casa de Joe's had, hands down, the best Mexican food in town.

"That'll work. I can get a taco salad there."

"Beautiful. We'll gather everyone there in a few days. Do you think Harry and Julie can make it?"

"If not, I can send the girls over to babysit. Hmm, I probably ought to ask Tori about this first. After all, this is pretty much about her."

Not really, but I didn't have the heart to point that out to him. Yes, the character looked, talked, and acted with the same mannerisms as Tori, Vance's wife, but that's where the similarities ended. After all, it's not like Tori was living in Ireland during the mid-nineteenth century.

Vance pulled out his cell.

"Hey, Tor, sorry to bother you at work. Got a minute to talk? No, there's nothing wrong. No, the girls are fine. No, I'm fine. Everything's fine. Jeez, woman, let me get a word in edgewise and you'll see why I called. It's about the book. Yes, that book. Yes, he finally asked the question. Hold on, I'm putting you on speakerphone."

"Zack?" Tori's voice asked. "Can you hear me?"

"I can, Tori. How are you today?"

"Doing much better if you're going to ask me what I'm hoping you'll ask me."

"Am I that transparent?" I laughed.

"You're going to ask me about a sequel? To the Irish book?"

"I was, yes. Jason Statham's fiancée is the latest celebrity to ask about the possibility of continuing the story, so I thought I'd run it by you guys first. Just be warned. We'd have some work to do."

"You make it sound like there'd be troubles with it," Tori said. I couldn't see her face, obviously, but I knew she was frowning. "What's wrong?"

I took Tori through the same spiel I gave Vance just a few moments ago. Even after listening to all the concerns I had, she was willing to do whatever it took to make a sequel worthy of the original. Plus, she said this had nothing to do about money. Personally, I think she was enjoying the fame that went along with it.

"We'll discuss it in detail this Friday," I promised. "If we can get everyone together, we'll have a brainstorming session."

"You're on, Zack. Thank you so much! You're the best!"

"Oh, I know it," I laughed.

"His head is already big enough," Vance complained. "No more compliments, okay?"

"Just you wait until Friday. Zack? You and Jillian are to order whatever you want. We're picking up the bill. For everyone."

"All right!" I exclaimed, as I sat up in my chair. "Now we're talking! Thanks, Tori!"

"Thanks, Tor," Vance moaned. "You didn't have to tell him that."

I heard Tori laugh and then Vance's cell went dark.

"Well, that backfired miserably."

"All depends on where you're sitting, pal," I told him.

Just then, Sherlock and Watson perked up. In fact, I'd say Sherlock was about ready to ...

"Woof!"

Surprised, both Vance and I turned to see what had caught his attention. In this case, it was *who*. Captain Nelson was standing on the other side of Vance's door, chatting with one of the officers on duty.

"Woof!" Sherlock repeated.

We watched as a look of surprise came across the captain's face. Looking left, then right, he finally turned to look behind him. Sherlock was standing at full attention, with both ears sticking straight up. Watson had adopted a similar stance.

"If it isn't my most prized detectives."

I stifled a laugh and looked back at Vance, who was in the process of rolling his eyes.

"I'd give you a treat if I had one," the captain said, as he approached the open door and held out a hand.

What happened next had Vance laughing out loud so hard that it almost brought the entire department to a standstill. It was my own fault, I guess. I had made the unfortunate decision of sitting in an office chair that just so happened to have wheels on it. What it was doing in Vance's office, I didn't know. What I *did* know was that both those corgis of mine could have easily been a team of draft horses in another life.

I was literally *yanked* out of the office and dragged, in reverse, toward the captain as both dogs lunged for him at the same time. It made quite a racket, as I bounced off walls, desks, filing cabinets, and anything else the corgis wove around. When I finally stopped moving, and the entire station had stopped laughing, I was able to turn my chair around and face front. There, of course, was the captain, who was staring at me as though I had escaped from Area 51.

"Well. That had to hurt, Mr. Anderson."

"Oh, that's what Advil is for. Sherlock, Watson, was that really necessary?"

"I don't have a treat for them," the captain was saying.

Vance stepped forward and presented two doggie biscuits. Captain Nelson took them, nodded at Vance, and promptly held them out to the dogs. Two corgi derrieres quickly sat. I watched the dogs munch on their treats as the captain walked away. However, both dogs were still staring at his retreating form.

"Have they ever fixated on the captain like that before?" Vance asked, coming up behind me. "I don't recall them ever doing that."

"That makes two of us," I said. "Come on, guys. We should really get going."

Neither dog budged.

"What's up with them?" Vance asked. "Do they want to follow him?"

"I'm not sure. What should I do? Give them some slack and see where they take us?"

Vance shrugged. "Why not?"

"You heard him, guys," I told the corgis. "What do you want me to see? Show me, would you?"

My dogs didn't need to be asked twice. Sherlock and Watson surged forward. It was all I could do to keep from bumping into people, tipping over potted plants, and so on. Intent on watching the show, Vance followed the three of us as we made our way through the station. Thankfully, we didn't have far to go.

"What now?" I asked, as we stopped before the captain's office, which was pretty much nothing more than a glass box. Granted, all the many windows had blinds, but they were currently open, no doubt so the captain could keep an eye on the activity level of the station.

"Is he in there?" Vance asked, as he leaned around me to see inside.

"Yeah, but it looks as though he's on the phone."

Captain Nelson was pacing in his office and gesturing wildly, as if to prove his point. The problem was, unless he was on a video call, it wasn't going to do any good. After a few moments, the captain looked up, saw that he was being watched, and motioned for us to come inside. Vance promptly excused himself and headed in the opposite direction.

"You guys had better be on to something," I softly muttered to the dogs, as I reached for the door handle.

Captain Nelson indicated I should close the door and have a seat. He still hadn't been able to pull himself away from the phone.

"Look, I cannot spare the manpower," the captain was saying. "My budget is stretched thin as it is, and I'm not going to ... no, we're not going to bother the lab with something as trivial as this. There's no need to take a sample. Look, I have to go. Something has come up and I'm needed elsewhere. Yes, I'll keep you posted if I find anything out. Thank you."

"I'm sorry," I began, as soon as the captain had replaced the receiver on the telephone. "Sherlock and Watson led me here, and I'm not sure why. But, you know what? You're busy, so why don't we just ..."

"You're not ditching me now, are you?" Captain Nelson asked, growing concerned. "I just used you as an excuse to get off the phone."

Oh. How was I supposed to respond to that?

"Umm, is everything all right?"

"What, that? Don't worry about it. The mayor's son is insisting he's being targeted by someone who only wants to make him look bad."

"Dare I ask in what way?"

"The little punk drives a Porsche, and he keeps getting it crapped on by a bunch of birds."

"How can someone be responsible for that?" I asked, as I tried to keep myself from snickering. "Does he think someone is following him with a bunch of caged birds and is releasing them only when he sees him parking?"

The captain let out a bark of laughter.

"Right? Anyway, he seems to think he has the authority to order me around, and if I don't comply, he whines to his mother, or finds some way to make me look bad."

"Sorry you have to deal with that," I offered.

Captain Nelson shrugged. "I can handle that peon. Now, this is the second time I've come across you today. Do you need something from me?"

I pointed at the dogs.

"They're the ones who alerted me to your presence earlier, and when you came this way, they *insisted* we follow you."

The captain sank into his chair and eyed the corgis, who were eyeing him back.

"They're staring at me. Why?"

"I have no clue. The only thing I can tell you is that you're a corgi clue now."

Captain Nelson blinked a few times and leaned forward to rest his elbows on his desk.

"Come again?"

I explained to the captain what a corgi clue meant, and that the simple act of taking your picture as you walked away mollified them. I told him that once we decided to leave, the dogs decided otherwise, and presto, here we were.

"You're working a case?" Captain Nelson asked. "How come I don't know anything about this?"

"Because Sherlock and Watson are investigating

something at my house," I clarified. "The hollow foundation. With the Civil War trunk."

The captain leaned back in his chair and nodded.

"I stand corrected. I *have* heard of this. Don't you have an archaeological team currently excavating the site?"

"I do, yes. They've found human remains, I'm sorry to say."

"From the Civil War," Captain Nelson guessed.

"It appears that way."

"What was in the trunk?"

"Well, I let Burt Johnson go through the contents. He found all kinds of things. Cartridge boxes, books, clothes, personal effects, and even a rusted saber."

"What are you planning on doing with all of that stuff?" the captain politely inquired.

Was it me, or did Captain Nelson sound like he was interested in these little pieces of history? As if reading my thoughts, I noticed both Sherlock and Watson, who had just settled to the floor, jump back to their feet and were now staring at the wall directly behind—and above—the captain's head. It wasn't a picture frame, but a shadow box. Inside was a collection of items I couldn't identify, but they looked old.

"Like it?" Captain Nelson asked, as he turned to see what had caught our attention. "They're all authentic relics from the Civil War period, too. I'm something of a collector."

That would explain his interest in the artifacts found at my old house.

"What do you have in the box? Are those buttons?"

The dogs were staring at the box as though it was filled with biscuits. Sighing, I took a picture.

"Buttons, medals, and a few patches," Captain Nelson explained, as he took the box off the wall and gently placed it on his desk. He motioned me over. "These three here, they came off an officer's coat. And just below those buttons, on the left, you'll find a set of field duties."

"A set of *what*?" I asked.

"Shoulder straps. Color denoted rank. Those straps are sky blue, which meant the owner of those straps was a member of infantry. I also have a couple of gold buttons, which came off an overcoat of some type. I don't know whose, unfortunately. You said you found some clothing?"

"Some type of shirt," I recalled. "Burt had an official name for it. It was old, and dirty, but in decent shape."

"Are you planning on letting Burt sell those items?"

"Probably. Look, if there's something you'd like, then let me know. I can see about setting something aside for you."

"Guns."

"Guns? No, to tell the truth, I haven't seen any thus far. Then again, it's been over twenty-four hours since I checked in with Professor Houston. He might have found a weapon or two by now. Did you know, the last time I talked to him, he stated they had found the remains from six different people? It's crazy. I'm beginning to think my winery used to be a burial ground."

"There's never a dull moment with you around, is there?" Captain Nelson asked, giving me a grin. "I would be in your debt if you happened across a pistol or a rifle."

I pulled out my phone.

"Well, let's find out, shall we? Give me just a moment. Professor Houston? It's Zack. Hey, I was calling to see how you guys are doing. How are things progressing? What's that? The number of human remains hasn't changed? That's definitely good. You found a what? A canteen. Huh. Wonder why it was buried? Look, I have a question. Someone asked me whether or not we've discovered any weapons. The only thing I could tell him was that we found a rusted cavalry sword. I ... oh? Is that so? Well, thanks to you, I get the honor of making someone's day. What's that? No, I haven't decided what I'm doing with everything yet."

"What did they find?" Captain Nelson whispered, his eyes sparkling with eagerness.

I held up a finger, indicating I needed him to wait. That was about the time I realized I was scolding the captain of the police, as if he had been a child caught passing notes in class, and in hindsight, it probably wasn't the best thing in the world to do. Then again, Captain Nelson hadn't objected, so I could only hope I wasn't going to hear about it later.

"Thank you for the update, Steve. I'll be by in a little while to see how everything is going. Good. Take care." Ending the call, I turned to the captain. "They found two rifles. The first was something called a Springfield rifled musket. The second was different. One of the grad students found out what it was by looking online: a Lorenz rifle. I have no idea what any of that means, but judging from the smile on your face, can I assume you've heard of both?"

"Indeed, I have. The Springfields were the gold standard of rifles used during the war. Those rifles were single shot, muzzle-loading guns which used percussion caps to fire."

"Percussion caps were found in the trunk," I confirmed.

"Authentic percussion caps. How about that? Anyway, I could go on, but I won't bore you with details."

"No worries. You can definitely have one. Now, I don't know what condition it's in, but if you ..."

"I'll take it!" the captain interrupted. A huge smile appeared on his face as he shook my hand. "You've made my day. Thank you. You mentioned a sword? Might you have any plans for it?"

"I may not care for guns," I said, "but I do love swords. Sorry, but I'll be keeping that one."

"Good for you. Again, thank you."

"You're welcome. Sherlock, Watson, can we head home now?"

The dogs rose to their feet, gave themselves a thorough shaking, and headed for the door without so much as looking back at the captain.

"Guess that means we're done. I'll keep you posted."

Captain Nelson nodded. "Please do."

Back in my Jeep, we had just turned onto Main Street when my phone rang. This time, it was Burt.

"I heard from Angelica, and thought you'd like to know."

"She found something? Already? That's awesome. All right, hit me with your best shot."

"The 4th Oregon Volunteer Infantry Regiment," Burt intoned, clearly reading from some notes he must've taken, "was stationed in Grants Pass after reports of rising hostilities between miners became prevalent in the area."

"The Oregon gold rush," I said. "We kinda figured it was related in some fashion."

"Right. Your particular regiment wanted to move closer to PV, supposedly with the intent to keep a closer eye on things."

"Again, it makes sense. After all, PV played a very significant part with this state's discovery of gold."

"Angelica found proof that repeated requests were made to relocate the 4th from Grants Pass to PV. Each time, however, it was denied."

This was definitely news to me. The soldiers wanted to move closer to the gold, asked for permission, and were denied? Clearly, with the discovery of what was left of the 4th in the foundation of my old house, a group of soldiers took it upon themselves to make the trip. Did that mean they all deserted? Maybe they assumed their request would be granted, and then decided to defy their orders and relocate their camp anyway?

Then again, they *were* found in a hollowed-out section of a house's foundation, so there had to be a reason why someone sought to conceal their presence. The question I had was, *who?* Who was the one who made the decision to build a house around the spot where a number of soldiers had lost their lives? For that matter, what had killed them? Had there been some type of mutiny in the ranks? Could there have been some type of environmental variable at play?

The more I discovered about this hidden encampment of soldiers, the more I realized that there was definitely something wrong.

SIX

Have you ever had good intentions, yet it would seem like the universe had other plans? By that, I mean, you have a project that you know has a deadline (like a book), and it has to be finished (like a book), and yet whenever you try to dedicate some time to get that work done, something happens? Well, that's what it felt like was happening to me all throughout the following day. I was back in Carnation Cottage, trying valiantly to keep my mind focused on my latest novel. However, between the attention-demanding corgis, my constantly ringing cell phone, and a wandering mind, I couldn't concentrate. Again. And boy-howdy, was it getting irritating.

I vowed some time ago to *never* get angry at my dogs for wanting some attention from me. There will come a day, I guarantee you, that you will look back at how you spent time with your beloved pets and be willing to trade anything to spend a few more moments with them. Therefore, the corgis knew that all they had to do to get a reaction out of their daddy was to show up at my desk with a ball (or toy) in their mouth and look at me with their large, soulful eyes. I personally don't care if I'm in my zone, or the middle of a conversation, or simply doing something else, when I see Sherlock and Watson wanting some attention from me, ninety-five percent of the time, they'll get it.

That's how the corgis were today. Every time I thought the dogs were settling down, whether with a toy or watching their special pet-friendly programming on television, they'd find their way into my temporary office. The latest instance happened just after three p.m. when the three of us had just returned from a walk around the neighborhood. I had thought an outing of just under two miles would have taken some of the steam out of their engines, but when I returned to my desk, in my peripheral vision, I noticed both dogs had just trotted back into the room. Watson, bless her little heart, had a tennis ball in her mouth.

Hoping the corgis were just seeing what I was doing, I opened my laptop, cracked open a fresh can of soda, and was preparing to start typing. Just as I did, Watson let out a piteous whine. Glancing down, I saw two sets of imploring canine eyes staring at me. Sighing, I closed the laptop's lid, pushed myself away from my desk, and pretended to stretch.

By this time, Sherlock and Watson were watching me like a hawk. Knowing what was about to happen, Sherlock started tip-tapping … make that hopping … wow, I don't know what to call it. He was wiggling so much that he simply couldn't stay still. Had he been standing on a hardwood floor instead of the bedroom's carpeted one, he'd be making a loud clicking noise.

Still doing my fake stretch, I leaned forward—while continuing to ignore both dogs—and made all kinds of noises. As expected, the dogs were unsure of what I was doing, so they started to head-tilt me. Surprising myself by moving as fast as I did, I snatched the yellow tennis ball out of Watson's mouth and bolted out of the room.

From the barks that followed, you'd think I just declared war on the Kingdom of Canines.

Ducking into the hall bathroom, I hid behind the door as the corgis tore by me going Mach I. Laughing hysterically, I sprinted in the opposite direction, toward the living room. Now, this is where I tell you that this room was supposed to have carpet as well, only it had been removed when Jillian purchased the house and had its hardwood floor restored to its former glory. My wife spared no expense in having the floor stripped, sanded, stained, sealed, and then polished. Then, she placed several (very expensive) decorative rugs around the room, giving the space an elegant and comfortable appearance at the same time.

Why do I tell you this? Well, seeing how I was currently living in this particular house, *and* I was trying to relax and work, I had kicked my shoes off. See where I'm going with this now? I hit the hardwood floor of the living room in my stockinged feet and turned into a newborn giraffe taking its first steps. Momentum carried me to the nearest oriental rug, only I was still moving and couldn't possibly stop. Together, rider and surfboard slid our way into the closest wall. I hit it so hard that I swear the entire wall was knocked off its foundation, and then—just like in the movies—a picture frame was knocked loose. Since it was the signed Thomas Kinkade painting I had purchased for Jillian during our Monterey trip, I knew I couldn't let it fall. Then again, I was off-balance and already in the process of falling, so at this point, I threw caution to the wind. Abandoning all reasoning and worries about hurting myself, I pretended I was a star volleyball player and had decided to martyr myself by trying to save an errant ball, only unfortunately for me, I was not wearing any protective gear.

Both knees slammed into the ground, bringing tears of pain to my eyes, but I didn't care. Twisting, I felt my back protest angrily, but again, I didn't have time to worry about it. There was the painting, moving as if everything was in slow-motion. But … *I caught it in time.* There will be no doghouse in my immediate future, thank you so much.

The front door opened and Jillian arrived home, humming a happy tune. She placed her purse on the kitchen counter, hung her keys on a set of pegs that had been installed for that exact purpose, and headed toward me. Without breaking stride, she plucked the painting from my hands and, tsking slightly, placed the picture back on the wall. Still humming her merry little tune, she stepped over my prone form and headed for the bedroom, intent —I knew—on changing into some comfier clothes.

You might be wondering what was wrong with my wife. Why would she ignore me when I was on the floor? Would she not have had the decency to ask if I was all right? Well, to answer those questions, I have to pose one of my own: what are the chances that this wasn't the first time she's found me in a situation like this? If your answer was *highly likely, Zachary,* then you'd be right.

"Hard at work or hardly working?" Jillian asked, as I limped down the hall, headed toward the bedroom.

"Oh, you know me. Your two dogs were wanting a little attention, that's all."

By the time I made it to the master bedroom, Jillian was already in a soft, fuzzy sweater (the woman was always cold) and a pair of black leggings. My wife finally turned to look at me, noticed the pain on my face, and automatically retrieved a bottle of ibuprofen from the bathroom medicine cabinet. From the way she opened the pill bottle and handed the meds over, you'd think this kind of thing happened on a regular basis.

"Here, you're getting four of them. No, don't argue. You're getting too old to be playing around on the floor. And those two are definitely *your* dogs."

"Playing on the floor wasn't my first intention," I grumbled, as I took the proffered pills and downed them once I filled a glass from the bathroom sink. "Believe it or not, I was trying to work, only …"

"… only the dogs wanted to play," Jillian guessed. She squatted next to the corgis and draped an arm around each of them. "You two need to go easier on your daddy. He's not a spring chicken anymore."

"Age jokes. That's just swell. What are you up to now?"

"I'm thinking I would find something on television, put my feet up, and maybe figure out something for dinner. If it's all the same to you, I really don't feel like cooking."

"I haven't hit my word goal yet," I announced, "so I'm not quite done writing for the day. I'd love to get another thousand or two words in. But, I'm all for skipping the kitchen tonight, too, and finding something that'll deliver."

"I'm on it," Jillian reported. "Go finish your book."

"I'll try."

With my wife kindly keeping the dogs occupied, I returned to my desk and opened my laptop. I had no sooner typed out a single paragraph when my fingers froze. For some reason, my mind drifted back to the case we were on, and no matter how hard I tried, it stayed there.

What had those soldiers been doing on my future property? Why would they have defied orders when they knew they should've stayed with the rest of their unit? Who made the decision to hide the burial site inside the foundation?

The more I looked for answers, the more I realized I had way more questions than solutions.

Forty-five minutes passed as I attempted to steer my attention back to my book. However, I ended up throwing in the towel. I think it was clear: until I started answering some of these pressing questions, my work was going to have to be put on hold. So, where do I start? Visiting the local museum? Did PV actually have one? Maybe I should swing by the library? What about a bookstore? Someone, somewhere, must have wondered what happened to these men. I just had to do a little digging.

"I think I need to head into town," I said, as I emerged from my makeshift office and entered the living room. "I've been thinking about the case, and I'll be honest. It's hard to think about the book when I know the remains of six people have been found on my property. I think I need to focus on this for a little while."

Jillian nodded. "Where are you going to go? The library?"

"I was thinking about checking out the

museum. PV played an important role in the start of Oregon's gold rush. Maybe I'll get lucky."

"I doubt it."

In the process of taking my keys down from the neat rows of pegs, I hesitated.

"And you say that *why*?"

"PV doesn't have a dedicated museum."

"Oh. Well, so much for that. Maybe I'll head to Dottie's."

Explaining who Dottie Hanson was requires a little bit of an explanation. The current owner of A Lazy Afternoon, my favorite bookstore in PV, is the only child of former owner Clara Hanson, a colorful character who met her end at the hands of my former archnemesis, Abigail Lawson. Clara was someone who lived by the motto *single and ready to mingle*. She was a widow, and was always on the lookout for the future Mr. Clara Hanson. Once she passed away, her estranged daughter, Dottie, made the move to PV and took over her mother's business. Since she didn't have any friends, or any other living relatives, Dottie seemingly attached herself to me and Jillian, and we've been fairly close ever since.

"That's a good idea. Umm, if you want me to come, I'll need to change."

"Do you want to come?" I asked.

"Is it bad that I don't?" Jillian returned.

I smiled at my wife. "It's a perfectly acceptable answer. You've put in your hours. You're in your comfies. Stay here, unwind, and watch the dogs. I'll be back in a bit."

Kissing her goodbye, I made it about four steps toward the door when Sherlock and Watson appeared in my path. They were apparently not too keen about staying home.

"Did you really think that was going to work?" Jillian laughed.

"Well, I tried. Come on, guys. You can come with me to Dottie's."

Twenty minutes later, the three of us were walking through A Lazy Afternoon's main entrance. This may have been a bookstore, but I could see that Dottie had expanded her offerings to include a wide selection of local products. Endcaps on her racks of books had been configured to display local honey, pamphlets, postcards, greeting cards, and other items from local businesses. I'd like to think this was Dottie's idea, but this had Jillian's influence written all over it.

"Hi Zack!" Dottie said, as she appeared around the corner from one of the racks of books. "Hey, I think you should know I'm out of the signed hardcover Ireland books. I ordered another shipment, so whenever you can make it over here to sign them, I'll have your pizza waiting for you."

It was an easy trade. Dottie supplies the books and the bribe, I provide my John Hancock on whatever book she wants to feature.

"You got it. Just let me know when you get them in. Listen, I was wondering something. Do you have any books on the Civil War? Or, more specifically, anything about the local connection to the Civil War?"

"You're talking about Pomme Valley's role in the Civil War?" Dottie asked, as she placed her hands on her hips and turned to face her store. There was only one other customer present, and he was currently looking at travel books. "That's a good question. Does this have anything to do with the remains found in your old house?"

"Wow, really? How do you know about that?"

"I heard it from Tammy, who heard it from Susan, who heard it from her roommate, Dori, who works as a bartender at Red Barn Tavern. One of the grad students was there last night."

"This really is a small town," I observed, laughing. "Anyway, you're right. I need to figure out why the remains of six soldiers were found inside the foundation."

"Well, my History section is right over there," Dottie said, pointing. "If there's one topic I'm not too familiar with, it'd be the Civil War."

The dogs and I followed Dottie around several racks until we came to a section that had some of the biggest hardcover books in the store. Stooping to read a few of the titles, I could see the largest was entitled *War*. I'll definitely pass on that one. Another was about war machinery. That one was about all the various fighter jets and their roles throughout history.

"Excuse me?"

Dottie and I looked up. Sherlock and Watson,

spooked by the sudden appearance of the older gentleman who had been perusing the Travel section, woofed a warning.

"Oh, I wouldn't hurt you, you big furballs," the elderly man said, as he leaned forward to present his hand. After each corgi gave the hand several tentative licks, the man straightened. "Hugh Martinson."

"Zack Anderson," I returned. "This is Dottie Hanson, owner of the store. Down there are …"

"… Sherlock and Watson," the man interrupted. "No introductions are necessary for them. They're the talk of the town."

"Is there something I can do for you, Mr. Martinson?" Dottie politely asked. "Are you looking for a particular book?"

"Actually, I thought I might be able to help you," the elderly gentleman said, offering both me and Dottie a smile. "I used to teach history, at SOU."

"Southern Oregon University," I said, nodding. "I can definitely picture you as a professor. Do you know something about the Civil War?"

"American wars are my specialty," Hugh proudly announced. "I've been fascinated with our country's history of warfare, and wrote several books on the subject. You had asked about Pomme Valley's role in the Civil War?"

I raised a hand. "I did, yes. What can you tell us?"

"That Pomme Valley's role was … *limited*, to say the least."

"That correlates with what I've heard thus far," I

said, sighing.

"You mentioned human remains were found on your property?" Hugh continued. "Buried within the foundation walls of your house?"

"Former house, but yes."

"Have you notified anyone about it?"

"As a matter of fact, I have a team from the University of Oregon currently excavating the site. Professor Houston and two of his grad students."

"Professor Houston?" Hugh repeated. "His name wouldn't be *Steve Houston*, would it?"

"As a matter of fact, it is. He told me he's been part of quite a few digs, including some lost golden city in Egypt."

"Steve was a student of mine. I was quite fond of him. Would you mind if I paid him a visit?"

Maybe it was because I have an active imagination, but several warning lights went off. I didn't know this guy, and what would be the odds of encountering someone who claims they know the person presently excavating a historical site on my land? Something didn't add up, and quite frankly, I was tired of it.

"I can see on your face that you don't trust my intentions," Hugh was saying. "It's okay. A personal visit isn't necessary. I just wanted to say hello."

I pulled out my phone and dialed a number.

"Zack? Is everything okay?"

"Hi, Steve. Listen, I'm at the local bookstore, looking for anything which could help me learn more about the soldiers you guys are currently digging up and I bumped into someone who claims to know you."

"Were," Steve corrected, chuckling lightly.

"What was that?"

"We finished excavating just a little while ago. We're cataloging what we found and we should be able to wrap things up by the end of the week. Wait. This person you found. He knows me?"

"Hello, Mr. Houston," Hugh announced, leaning over my phone. His voice had strengthened itself and I could easily imagine sitting in a lecture hall, listening to that voice explain that day's assignments. "It's been a long time. Still drink those disgusting energy drinks you favor so much?"

We heard the telltale *clink* as an aluminum can was hastily set upon a metallic table.

"Professor Martinson? No way!"

"Hello, kid. It's good to hear from you."

"What are you doing in Pomme Valley, sir?"

"I was just passing through and was thinking about retiring here. I had stopped off at the local bookstore, to see what selections they have."

"And?" Dottie quietly whispered.

Hugh looked over at the store owner and nodded. "It's very encouraging. Listen, my dear boy, I hear you're excavating a site. Well, *excavated* a site. My interest is piqued. Can I come by and see your work?"

"I'd be honored, sir," Professor Houston said,

sounding very much like he had regressed twenty years. "Zack? Do you mind?"

"Not at all. I'll give him directions to my house. But, before I let either of you go, can I ask something? Mr. Martinson, are you able to help us out in some fashion? You approached us, remember?"

"Oh, silly me. Of course, I forgot. I noticed a book earlier that could probably be of some assistance to you."

Dottie perked up. "Oh? And which one was that?"

Hugh turned to point at a nearby rack of books which was, conveniently enough, the History section. "*The Enemy Never Came: The Civil War in the Pacific Northwest*. There's a wonderful section in there about Oregon, and if I'm not mistaken, it mentions something about this state's gold rush. I also remember seeing a list of names."

I snatched the book from the shelf. "You're kidding. Dottie, I'll take it. Hugh, it's been a pleasure talking to you. Think you can find your way over to the excavation site?"

Hugh gave me a gracious smile and held up his phone. "Of course. Then again, if I can't, well, I'll cheat. Good day to you both."

I squatted low to give the corgis a scratching behind their ears as Dottie was ringing up my book. That's when I heard her sigh. Straightening, I looked at the twenty-nine-year-old store owner and waited for an explanation. Dottie handed me the bag with my book, but not before looking up into my face.

"What?"

"You tell me. I just heard you sigh. Is everything all right?"

"Oh, sure, sure. Everything's fine."

"Like I'm gonna believe that," I said, crossing my arms. "Out with it, woman. What's the matter? Are you all right?"

"Yeah, I am, it's just that … well, Zack, it's nothing."

It was my turn to sigh. Placing the sack with my book on the counter, I turned to look at the young woman who had become a close, personal friend. I held up my left hand.

"I'm married. I know that particular sigh. It says, there's something I want to say, but I don't know how it's going to make me look." If I wasn't too far off the mark, I'd say Dottie blushed. "And now I'll say it's something personal. If it's a, uh, *personal* problem, well, then, I'll get Jillian on the line for you."

Dottie burst out in a fit of giggles. "No, it's nothing like that. It's just that … well, here in Pomme Valley, it's so quiet. Nothing ever happens around here."

"If you're looking for excitement," I began, "then look to the east. Medford is only fifteen minutes away."

"That's not the type of excitement I was looking for."

My eyebrows shot up. If possible, Dottie's blush deepened.

"Omigod, that's not what I mean. I … oh, just dig me a hole and bury me, would you?"

I finally caught the gist of what Dottie was trying to say. I think.

"You're, ah, lonely, is that it?" Dottie wouldn't look me in the eye. Her face was as red as a fire truck. "Have you asked Jillian to set you up? She knows everyone in town, remember?"

"I haven't had the courage," Dottie groaned.

"I'll ask her for you," I promised.

"Just … don't make it creepy," Dottie pleaded.

"Tell you what. I'll just tell her you mentioned you wanted to talk to her. Deal?"

Dottie stared at the floor and scuffed at it with the toe of her sneaker. I waited a few moments before continuing.

"If this is an uncomfortable subject, then I don't have to say anything, you know."

"Oh, good. Maybe you shouldn't."

"But … now that I know …"

"Oh, God. You wouldn't."

"You're not happy, Dottie," I said, as I looked at the blushing store owner. "Jillian is just the person to take care of this. Trust me."

"All right," Dottie finally said, unable to meet my eyes. "My love life is in your hands. Er, *her* hands."

Loading the dogs into the Jeep, we headed home.

"That didn't take long," Jillian reported, from the sofa. "Find something useful?"

I held up the sack. "I think so."

I gave my wife a recap of everything that had transpired at the store, finishing with Dottie's embarrassing admission she was, well, seeking companionship.

"That must have been a fun conversation. Of course, I know several eligible bachelors. I'll be more than happy to make some arrangements."

"I think she'd be in your debt," I said, as I kicked off my shoes and sank down next to her. Pulling the book out of the bag, I showed Jillian my recent purchase. "I can only hope Hugh Martinson was right. Hey, this is promising. There's an entire chapter devoted to Pomme Valley. How 'bout that?"

"All about PV? Really?"

I flipped to chapter nine and held the book out. Jillian took it and skimmed the page.

"Anything useful?" I hopefully asked.

"Nothing new. The main fort appeared to be in Grants Pass ..."

"... which we knew," I interrupted.

"Right. All the soldiers' infantrymen were local recruits from the Portland area. The officers weren't, of course. They all came from the east coast."

"Anything about the gold rush?"

"Not on these two pages. I'll speed-read a few others."

Sherlock and Watson jumped onto the couch next to us. Sherlock made it to me first and wedged himself between me and Jillian. Watson looked at me for a few moments before moving close to my left leg and flopping over, as if someone had pushed her. Scratching her back, Watson fidgeted a few times before giving up and rolling onto her back. Sherlock, in the meantime, was also fidgeting, but his only intent was to force himself further between me and Jillian. Once he had smooshed himself as far down as he would go, he then forcefully stretched his stumpy legs out, which had the effect of making Jillian scooch over so that he'd have more room.

Pleased with the effort, Sherlock looked up at me and smiled.

"I've got something," Jillian announced, several minutes later. "I have … well, I think I have the names of the soldiers who mutinied."

"Deserted," I corrected, "and you're kidding!"

"I'm not. Look. Four squads were assigned to the 4th Oregon Volunteer Infantry Regiment. It wasn't many, but for the time and area, it was enough. One squad, it says here, was lured away by the discovery of gold in nearby Pomme Valley. The squad even has a name."

"Let's hear it."

"Slippery Jack."

"Slippery Jack? I can only assume it meant something to them."

"I would agree. For whatever the reason, it's the name this group of men gave themselves. The SJ squad petitioned for … Zachary, What's the matter?"

"SJ! Of course! Wow, this is starting to make sense."

"*What* is?" Jillian wanted to know.

"SJ," I repeated. "I've seen those two letters before. I figured it was the owner of the trunk. Burt found a small oval tag on that trunk. It had SJ on it. Slippery Jack. I wonder what that's supposed to mean?"

Jillian spread her hands. "I don't have an answer for you, I'm sorry."

"It's okay. Now, these men? They had names?"

"I don't know how many of this SJ squad disappeared," Jillian began, "but we know it's at least six of them. Hmm, that's interesting."

"What is?" I asked.

Jillian tapped the page she was reading. More specifically, she tapped a text box that was shaded a different color from the rest of the passage.

"It says here that one in five soldiers in the Union army ended up deserting, and that number drops to one in three for the Confederates."

"One in five?" I repeated. "That's surprising."

"One in three for our southern boys," Jillian added. "Okay, here are the names. Ready?"

"Let's hear them."

"Are you going to write them down? I thought maybe you could give the names to Professor Houston when you see him next."

"Good idea, only the university's team is pretty much done excavating. They said they'll be gone by the end of the week."

"Did they find anything else?"

"I don't know." My notebook appeared. "Whenever you're ready."

Jillian returned her attention to the book. "It looks like the leader of the SJs was one Sgt. William O'Henry."

"Sounds like a nice, solid name for an officer."

"Then, we have Pfc Caleb Johnson."

"Wait a moment. P-F-C, what does that stand for?"

Jillian was silent as she considered.

"Private First Class."

"I like it. Please, continue."

"There's Pfc Ryan Nelson, Pfc Bartholomew Thompson, Pfc Darryl Jones, Pfc Henry Woodson, Pfc Benjamin Wilson, Pfc Josiah Milton, Pfc ..."

"How many more are there?" I said, exasperated. "I thought we were only looking for six names!"

"These are the names of the missing men," Jillian pointed out. "I think it just means that they never made it here, to PV."

"And what could have stopped them?" I asked, bewildered. "It's not like a journey from Grants Pass to PV would be fraught with peril."

"Are you kidding? Back then, there was the threat of Indian attacks, jealous miners, bandits, and even wild animals. I'm actually surprised that many made it to your house."

"It really makes you wonder," I said, leaning back on the sofa and petting both my dogs at the same time. "What drove those men to abandon their posts? No, scratch that. Clearly, it was the thought of all that gold, just waiting to be found. The problem I have is, well, yes, back then, PV was a decent distance away from Grants Pass. But, we're talking about desertion. That's something the US Government doesn't take lightly. If you're going to desert, then wouldn't you want to put as much distance as possible from the people you've deserted?"

"Well, you're the storyteller," Jillian said, as she placed the book on the coffee table and faced me. She stroked Sherlock's fur and looked straight at me. "Can you come up with a plausible scenario based on all the facts of this case?"

"All right. Challenge accepted, woman. Let's see. Let's start by assuming the SJ squad knew they wouldn't be going far. That is, not that far away from Grants Pass. Could they have been driven out?"

Jillian tapped the book with her foot, making my new purchase thump loudly on the table. Both corgis gave a little jump and then, in unison, turned to give me the stink eye.

"I didn't do that. She did. Scowl at her, would you?"

"I can't imagine an entire squad would have been driven out of the fort, and there wouldn't be any mention of it. What else do you have?"

"Well, what about relocating the squad due to a misunderstanding, or miscommunication, with someone at their headquarters?"

"You mean something like … they thought they heard one thing, but were given something else?"

"Exactly."

"Easy enough to explain the confusion with one person," Jillian said, "but with a dozen?"

"True. What about—and I know this is impractical—the SJ squad applied for permission to relocate, which we know they did, but they expected it would be approved. Therefore, instead of waiting for the permission they thought they'd be receiving, they collectively relocated, figuring they were already in the clear. What do you think?"

"My brother, Josh, is a Marine, as you know. He's always telling me how devoted he and his men are in serving the greater good. No soldier is going to abandon their post unless they're given specific orders to do just that."

"That leaves us with mutiny," I said, shaking my head.

"No, that means we're left with deserters," Jillian corrected. "Mutiny is where there's a challenge to the authorities, which typically leads to a rebellion of some type."

"That might've happened here," I insisted.

Jillian pointed at the book. "But, it isn't listed in there, is it? No, I think they simply deserted their posts for nothing more than greed."

I skimmed through the names I had written in my notebook and stopped on the third one. Pfc Ryan Nelson. Nelson? I happened to know a Nelson, and that was one Captain Nelson, of the PVPD. And there's one with another familiar name: Pfc Darryl Jones. There *is* a police officer with that last name, but then again, Jones had to be one of the most popular surnames in present times. It could be just a coincidence. Wilson, Milton, and Quinn. Did I know anyone with those last names?

"Penny for your thoughts?"

I looked at my wife and held the notebook up.

"I was just looking at the names and wondering which six were buried in my house. More than anything, I want to know who did it, and why."

"Tell you what," Jillian said, taking my hand. "It's getting late. Why don't we pay a visit to the library tomorrow, and if necessary, maybe the museum? I don't have anything pressing, so I can come with you."

I formed a T with my hands.

"Hang on a second. Time out. Didn't you already tell me there wasn't a museum here, in PV?"

"I said there wasn't a *dedicated* museum in PV. But, there just so happens to be a part-time museum, which is only open for the summer. The person who runs it ..."

"... is a friend of yours," I finished for her, rolling my eyes. "Or, the museum is housed in a building you own?"

Jillian winked at me. "Maybe."

* * *

The following morning, the two of us, along with Sherlock and Watson, walked hand-in-hand into the library. In case you're wondering, I normally wouldn't bring the dogs into a library like this, but I've been pulled aside so many times, assuring me the dogs were welcome pretty much everywhere we went, that it's become routine to bring them with me. Even the majority of the restaurants along Main Street were pet friendly, provided our furry companions kept to the exterior terraces.

"Good morning, Mrs. Anderson," a middle-aged woman greeted, as we walked by the check-out counter. "And Mr. Anderson, it's good to see … oh! You have your dogs! Millicent, come, look! Sherlock and Watson are here!"

As one, the group of older ladies came hurrying around the counter to begin heaping their adoration upon the corgis. Sherlock and Watson, for their part, absolutely loved the attention.

Catching the eyes of one of the workers, I beckoned her to the counter.

"Yes, Mr. Anderson? How can I help you today?"

"What do you have in the way of the US Civil War and the part PV might have played in it?"

"I'd better get you Mrs. Plunkett."

Mrs. Plunkett was the eighty-three-year-old head librarian. She had long, white hair—typically braided—so that it fell halfway down her back, and usually she wore sharp two-piece business suits one would expect to find at an executive office. She also wore a thin, black wire frame pince-nez when she was behind a computer, and when she was being addressed, she tended to look down her nose at whatever request was made of her.

Thankfully, she and Jillian are good friends.

"Mrs. Anderson, delighted to see you today," the librarian announced, as she appeared from within the back room and approached the counter. "Mr. Anderson. What can I do for you?"

Jillian looked at me and inclined her head. That's just great. For some reason, this particular lady intimidated the heck out of me. I think I remember hearing she was an elementary teacher a number of years ago, and I can easily picture her in that role. Can't imagine there was much backtalk in any of her classes.

"We're researching the Civil War, and the effects it had on this area," I began. "Is there anything you can tell us about it, or perhaps, point us toward a book?"

"The Civil War," Mrs. Plunkett said, closing her eyes for a few moments. "Believe it or not, the war had a profound effect on our area."

My eyes widened.

"I can see this surprises you, Mr. Anderson," Mrs. Plunkett said, offering me a thin smile. The smile deepened and became more genuine when she looked at my wife. "Would you like to hear how?"

Jillian nodded. "I would personally *love* to hear this."

"That makes two of us," I said, raising a hand.

"How do you think PV was formed?" the librarian suddenly asked, surprising us both.

I noticed both dogs had straightened, as though they were now listening to what was being said.

"Are you suggesting Civil War soldiers were responsible for forming Pomme Valley?" I asked, certain I had heard that wrong.

"That's exactly what I'm saying," Mrs. Plunkett said, nodding. "There were obviously people living in the area, so when there were enough of them, our little town was established."

"And you know for a fact," I said, "that the people who were living in this area were soldiers?"

"I'd say fifty-fifty," Mrs. Plunkett admitted.

"And who were the other fifty?" Jillian wanted to know.

"Miners."

"The gold rush," I said, nodding. "That makes sense. No offense, ma'am, but as a writer, I have to ask about the source of your information. Is it word of mouth?"

"The local paper. We have a collection dating back to the very early 1900s. Sometimes I read them during my down time. I find it utterly fascinating learning how people lived in the late nineteenth and early twentieth centuries. In fact, I was reading a copy dated from January of 1905, I believe. The papers are filled with stories about Civil War veterans and their families. The same goes for the mining community. Claim jumping was such a huge problem back then that the only things the poor miners could do was stake a claim, and then tell the paper about it so everyone knew what *wasn't* available. Shall I fetch a couple issues?"

I looked down at the corgis. Sherlock was sitting on his haunches and watching the librarian very closely.

"Yes, please. That'd be great."

"I'll be just a moment."

Ten minutes later, we were crowded around one of the library's many white tables, watching as Mrs. Plunkett set several yellowing papers in front of us. There wasn't too much to see. Each of the three issues she brought was no more than five or six pages. The print had to be half the size of a regular newspaper, and the photos were so grainy and blurry that you almost couldn't make out what was depicted.

Jillian took the first.

"Let's see. This one is dated January 8th, 1901. There's talk of record snowfall. The milkman's truck became stuck and had to have a local farmer, with a team of horses, pull it out. There was also mention of an upcoming Valentine's Day party at the courthouse, requiring formal attire."

"They sure knew how to party, didn't they?" I joked.

"For them, that was probably the ultimate outing," Jillian argued. "It was a chance to dress in your finest and enjoy the day."

We didn't find too much in the second issue, but in the third, we hit the jackpot. The paper was dated May 4th, 1907. In it was an article about the opening of the historic Carriage House Inn, which I knew was the large white building located near the high school. There were several included pictures, but I only had eyes for one. The larger picture depicted a ribbon cutting ceremony, with a middle-aged couple holding a slightly-larger-than-normal set of scissors. Their names were Mr. and Mrs. Ryan Nelson.

My eyes lit up as I recognized the name from the list of the SJ squad. But, just to be certain, I double-checked. Jillian tapped her finger on the tiny caption.

"Mrs. and Mrs. Ryan Nelson. I wonder if they're related to Captain Nelson?"

I showed Jillian my notebook. "Hon, this is it! Look! Ryan Nelson was from the Slippery Jack squad. This proves there were survivors!"

"I'd say this proves that, not only were there survivors," Jillian was saying, "but that Mrs. Plunkett is right. The soldiers played an integral part in the creation of our town!"

"Slippery Jack squad?" Mrs. Plunkett repeated, shaking her head. "That's the second time I've heard that name this week."

Both of us looked up.

"It is?" I asked, growing excited. "Can I ask under what circumstances was this particular group of men brought up before?"

"Someone was researching them, too. Trying to find survivors, I believe."

"Do you remember who was asking?" Jillian asked.

After a few moments, the librarian was shaking her head. "I'm sorry, I don't remember. I get a lot of requests at that counter."

My phone rung at that exact moment, earning me a frown from Mrs. Plunkett.

"Hey, Steve, I take it everything is all …?"

"We have a problem!" the professor interrupted. His voice was terse and I could clearly tell the good professor wasn't going to give me good news.

"What's going on?" I nervously asked.

"We just came back from lunch and discovered someone had broken into our van. Zack, we've been robbed!"

SEVEN

"W ho in the world would want to steal human remains?" I grumbled, as I wove the Jeep through traffic on the way back to Lentari Cellars. "The rifles I can understand. Clean those things up and you could probably sell them online."

"Someone clearly wasn't happy with those remains being unearthed after all this time," Jillian added.

"Yeah, but who?" I wanted to know. "Someone from town, or perhaps, someone from out of town?"

"Like someone from the university?" Jillian asked, frowning. "I can't imagine those remains having too much historical significance."

"The one positive side to this is that we must be getting closer to some answers," I decided. "We've got someone spooked. I just wish I knew *who*."

"Does Vance know about the robbery yet?"

"I sent him a text message. He let me know he was just getting out of the car. You know,

I'm really surprised the archaeological team didn't have everything secured."

"Why would you say that?"

"Well, I've seen their operation. I watched them set everything up. Their lab pretty much consists of a pop-up tent with sidewalls. Who knows how long they were stored in that tent before moving it to their van."

"They're professionals. I highly doubt that they left anything of importance in that tent."

"I'm just saying that the whole town probably knows what they've found during this excavation. And that van—probably wouldn't take much to break into it, either."

When we pulled up to what was left of my old house, I could see that Vance was, indeed, already there, along with two patrol cars. I saw Professor Houston talking with Vance and one other officer. The second, a policeman I recognized as Officer Jones, was visible inside the tent.

Hearing car doors slam closed, Vance looked up, saw me approach, and said something to the professor. Moments later, he was hurrying over to me.

"Hey, Zack. Jillian. Funny running into you two here."

"Hey, pal," I returned. "So, let me guess. Someone looking to make a quick buck stops by and helps himself to whatever is in the van? For that matter, was anything left in the tent?"

Vance shook his head.

"The tent hadn't been disassembled yet, and as you can imagine, it wouldn't be difficult to gain access. There was nothing of value in there. All the equipment and relics, including the remains, had been secured in their van."

With that, my friend pointed at the white step van parked nearby with the university's symbol painted on the door.

"What you're telling me is that everything was lined up, nice and convenient, inside the van, and our burglar helped himself."

Vance motioned for me to follow him. Jillian took Sherlock's leash from me and, together, we all headed toward the white step van. As we approached, I could see something long, shiny, and metallic sticking out of the door panel on the passenger side.

"They slim-jimmed the door," Vance explained. "Once inside, they simply unlocked the rest of the doors through the power locks feature and then helped themselves."

"How much did they get?" I groaned. "All of it, right?"

Vance motioned for the professor to join us. Steve refused to look me in the eyes.

"Tell them what you told me, Doc."

Steve finally looked up. "I am so sorry, Mr. Anderson. We shouldn't have left the van here. We just figured that, out in the open like this, it should be safe."

"It should've been safe," I muttered. "I don't

like knowing someone trespassed on my property and helped themselves to everything in your van. Where's Caden? Is he here? I see his car over there."

Lentari Cellars' master vintner appeared, looking stressed and *highly* irritated.

"I think this was a professional job," Caden said, as he approached. "The first thing I did was check the security system. Four different cameras showed a pickup truck pull in."

"What color?" Vance asked, as he whipped out his notebook.

Caden pointed up. "Look at the sky. It's just past sunset. The cameras lose their color capabilities once the sun goes down."

Frowning, I looked up. "Our cameras? They lost the ability to record in color? Since when? I have half a mind to call up the company and give them a piece of my mind!"

Jillian placed a calming hand on my shoulder to restrain me. "That won't be necessary, dear. I believe what Caden neglected to say is that the loss of color means the camera had switched to night mode, which uses infrared. When recording on the infrared spectrum, color becomes impossible."

I looked at Vance. "Did you know this?"

"Would you believe me if I said yes?"

I shook my head. "So, I'm not the only one. Wow. So, Caden, what you're saying is that we have no idea what color the pickup was. Do we know the make or model?"

"It looked like an older Chevy truck," Caden said.

"My grandfather had something similar when I was little."

"Chevy, older model. Can you narrow it down to a decade?"

"Umm ... the eighties?"

"It's not the greatest, but at this point, anything helps. Caden, what about the driver? What did he, or she, look like?"

"They were wearing an old-fashioned ski mask," Caden said. "I couldn't see any features."

"Male, female, tall, short, heavy, or lean?" Vance continued, without looking up from his note-taking.

"Let me think. I'd say male. And tall. Oh, he was skinny. Very skinny. Made me think of Ichabod Crane."

Vance nodded, but couldn't suppress the grin that formed.

"It helps. What was the time-stamp on the video? When did this happen?"

"We had left for the day," the professor explained. "Since it looked as though we were going to wrap this up much earlier than expected, I was taking Noel and Bobbi out for a beer. And before you ask, Detective Samuelson, both are legally allowed to do so."

Vance nodded once.

"How much did they make off with?" I wanted to know. "Did they get everything?"

"Well, not quite everything," Steve contradicted. "Out of the seven containers that were there, only three were stolen."

"Let me guess. The guns? Shirts? All the personal items?"

"Actually, only one of the rifles was taken. The guns were placed in separate containers, and I can tell you that they weren't covered, or anything like that. No wrappings or packaging. Nothing was concealed. If you lifted the lid, you'd see it right away."

"Why did you separate the rifles?" Vance asked. "Did you suspect something was going to happen to them?"

"Container number four," Noel answered, as he and the female grad student appeared next to the professor's side. "Bobbi and I were cataloging the items, and once they were notated, they were packed. We were on the fourth container, and that's including the items Mr. Anderson returned from the local antique store, when we ran out of room. It was the last item besides the bones, so the rifle started container five, as did the remains. Oh, and the sword, too."

"This theft was definitely not motivated by money," Vance decided. "I would have thought the antique weaponry would've been the first things to be taken. Professor Houston? You said you could give me a rundown on what was taken? Now is as good a time as any."

Professor Houston nodded and pulled out a folded piece of paper. "Right. Let's see. Of the seven containers we have, you now know three of them were taken."

Vance held up a hand. "Just a minute. Storage containers. Can you tell me how big they are?"

Professor Houston nodded. "I'm sure you know the kind I mean. They're big, black, very sturdy, and have yellow lids."

"The heavy black storage containers you can get from those huge discount warehouse stores," I said, nodding.

"Yes. Oh, look. I stand corrected. I thought they only had the one rifle and the remains. I'm glad I looked. Okay, the three containers held the remains of the soldiers, one of the rifles, a collection of coinage, some bullets, percussion caps, and one decaying jacket."

"I didn't know about the jacket," I confided to my wife.

"It was only recently found," Noel explained. "We had finished all quadrants but the one half-sized section, and we were prepared to leave it. We hadn't found anything in a few days, but Bobbi persevered, and what do you know? She was right to check."

"I think it was clear someone wanted those remains," I said. Vance nodded his agreement. "I just don't know who could have done it."

"They must mean something to someone," Vance decided.

"But why?" I demanded. "And by who? As far as I'm aware, we haven't spooked anyone."

"That you know of," Steve pointed out.

"True. I also should point out that these remains are over a hundred-fifty years old. I'm starting to think that whomever is worried about us finding something has blown this way out of proportion."

Vance finished taking notes and looked at the archaeologist.

"Have you ever had artifacts taken from a dig before?"

Steve shrugged. "It's happened before, yes."

"More than one time?"

"Yes."

"Could this be nothing more than kids playing a prank on you?"

Steve shook his head. "I usually deal with grave robbers. Or relic hunters. Any time there's a chance to make a buck, we have to be careful."

"And what you've found here," Vance continued, "is it considered valuable?"

"The remains? Hardly."

"What about the rifle I heard you mention. How valuable would that be?"

Professor Houston shrugged. "I don't know, detective. Maybe it's worth, say, a thousand dollars? Please remember, a second rifle, in even better condition, was left behind."

"That's true," Vance had to admit. "All right, I think it's safe to say I agree with all of you. This robbery has nothing to do with money. Zack, I know you and the dogs have been working on this. If you, or Sherlock and Watson, have any ideas about who could've done this, you're to let me know as soon as possible, okay?"

I heard the corgis shuffling about by my feet. Glancing down, I saw that Sherlock was sitting on his haunches and staring at the tent. At the same time, Watson turned to look at her packmate, then up at me, and after a few moments, she also turned to look at the temporary lab set up by the university personnel.

"Who's in there?" I wanted to know.

Vance turned to look. "Just one of the guys. I asked him to take a quick look around. Why? Is Sherlock watching the tent?"

I stepped out of the way and pointed at the dogs.

"Sure looks that way."

"Jonesy? Come out of there for a second, would you?"

The lanky form of Officer Jones, a policeman I've met on numerous occasions, appeared at the flap that was used as a door and gave my detective friend a curious look.

"There's nothing to worry about," Vance told the officer, as he caught sight of the concerned look on Officer Jones' face. "I just need to check something. Could you give Trujillo a hand?"

Officer Francisco Trujillo, or Franco as he was known to everyone in the department, was currently processing the ground surrounding the big step van. Hearing his name called, he looked up, saw his fellow policeman, and waved him over. The dogs, oddly enough, tracked Jones over to the white van. Looking at Vance, I could see him studying Jones' retreating form, too. My detective friend made eye contact with me and then looked pointedly at my phone. Sighing, I pulled my cell, snapped a picture, and waggled it in front of the dogs. I didn't need to bother. As soon as the picture was taken, the dogs lost interest.

"What was that all about?" Vance softly asked. "Why are Sherlock and Watson staring at cops? We sure as heck didn't do this."

"I took a picture," I told Vance, holding up my phone. "It'll make sense sooner or later. Speaking of which, I'm really looking forward to going through all these clues with everyone."

Vance nodded. "I forgot. It's Friday night. Casa de Joe's. We'll be there."

Casa de Joe's might not sound like an authentic Mexican restaurant, and it certainly wasn't run by a Mexican family. The owner, one Joe Cantolli, just so happened to be Italian. I found out later that he had married into a Mexican family and decided to open a restaurant in picturesque Pomme Valley. That was back in 1994. Everything, from the chips and salsa, to the enchiladas, and even their margaritas, was the best in town. Frankly, if it wasn't for Sarah's Pizza Parlor, I think we would be eating here on a weekly basis. Oh, wait. There was also Marauder's Grill, which would be a carnivore's ultimate paradise. There's also ... all right, I'll stop. There's a reason why I'm always complaining about having to drop a few pounds.

As I mentioned earlier, we would typically pick

Sarah's Pizza Parlor whenever the dogs and I were working a case and wanted to get everyone together. We'd all choose to order our favorite pizzas while we pondered over the purpose of the pics. One of the reasons I was glad we weren't going to Sarah's this time around was ... well, it was because of Vance.

I don't know if it's because of his age (he recently turned forty), or maybe it's because he enjoys grossing us out, but lately, my detective friend has been coming up with the most bizarre combination of ingredients to put on a pizza. I mean, we're talking some super nasty crap I wouldn't touch with a ten foot pole. To give you an example, the pizza that started this all off was a disgusting mix of peanut butter and tomato, doused with tabasco sauce. It was enough to clear the table, but we've since learned that as long as Vance sits near the door, then the putrid stench is kept to a minimum.

"I know what you're thinking," Vance chuckled. "You're glad we're not going out for pizza. Well, it's too bad. I do have a few other variations to try."

"Got it in one, pal. We all think you're nuts, by the way. What happened with your stomach? Still bothering you? Because, if it wasn't before, I'm sure it is now."

"Don't knock 'em until you try 'em. And it's starting to feel better, thank you very much."

"That's good. Think I'll still bring the Rolaids, just in case."

"Hey, let me ask you something. Provided they're recovered, what are you going to do with those two guns? Did you say the captain wanted one?"

"I saw that he was a history buff," I said, as we slowly walked the grounds surrounding the tent and van. "I promised him one."

"What about the other?" Vance asked, unable to hide his eagerness.

"Not you, too. Are you telling me you want the other one?"

"Get those guns cleaned up and they'd look fantastic on a wall," Vance said, closing his eyes with a smile. After a few moments, they opened. "I know you hate guns, pal, so I'm pretty sure you weren't planning on displaying them."

"Guilty as charged," I admitted. "The cavalry saber? That's another story. I'm all about the swords and daggers."

"Figured you would be. So, um, er, about that rifle …?"

"You can have it. You're right. I have no need for it. Provided it's returned."

"You rock, buddy. Thanks."

The dogs and I hung around the scene until Vance and the other officers finished their investigation. I even led the corgis around the perimeter, but neither of the dogs picked up on anything, meaning there wasn't anything there to investigate. Loading their Majesties into the Jeep, I followed my detective friend to the police station, and together, we headed toward Captain Nelson's office. Seeing us approach, he waved us inside. As was typical with him, the captain was on the phone.

"Yes, ma'am. I can totally see where he's coming from, but even you have to hear how ridiculous that sounds. Why in the world would a flock of birds be targeting his car? No, ma'am, I don't believe anyone has trained a bunch of birds to do their business on shiny red sports cars. Yes, ma'am, I know what happens to an automobile's paint if bird sh—, er, pardon me, ma'am. Everyone knows what bird feces will do to paint. Yes, ma'am, feel free to call anytime. You're welcome."

The captain replaced the phone's handset and looked up at Vance.

"Detective. Mr. Anderson. Oh, the dogs are here. I really need to see about keeping some treats in my desk. How are you two doing, you little fluffballs?"

Sherlock and Watson were wriggling so bad that I'm surprised they didn't flop over and ... never mind. There they go.

"Detective, do you have an update regarding the theft at Mr. Anderson's place?"

"Only that it doesn't appear to be motivated by money. Only one of the rifles was taken."

Alarmed, the captain looked at me.

"Don't worry," I assured the head of police. "The one that remains is yours. If we get the other one back, then it goes to him."

Captain Nelson gave Vance an appraising stare. "You, too? What's your motivation?"

"Just an enthusiast," Vance insisted.

A notion occurred. "Captain, can I ask you a question?"

I was given an exasperated wave of the hand, as though I alone was making the day unbearable with all my questions. "Are you related to a Private Ryan Nelson?"

In response, the captain turned to point at his collection of badges, buttons, and medals.

"Those all came from my great-great-grandfather's uniform, one Private First Class Ryan Nelson."

Grinning, I turned to Vance. "I knew it. They're related after all."

"Why do you want to know that?" the captain asked.

"Well, his outfit called themselves the SJ squad, or Slippery Jack squad. Ever hear of it?"

The captain shook his head no.

"It's never come up. Why do you ask?"

"This particular squad broke off from the 4th and made their way here, to PV," I explained. "Against orders."

"And you're telling me my ancestor is one of these deserters?" Captain Nelson carefully asked, frowning.

"It would appear that way. We think he might be one of the six deceased soldiers found in the remains of my old house."

"Impossible," Captain Nelson argued. "My ancestor is one of our town's founding fathers. He started—and built—Carriage House, here in town. His was the first inn to offer rooms to emigrants."

I looked at Vance, and then down at the dogs. "Well, there's one name we can cross off the list."

"What list?" the captain asked. He held out a hand. "May I see it?"

I nodded. "Sure. This list contains the names of the SJ squad, everyone who disappeared from their posts back at the base in Grants Pass."

Captain Nelson took my notebook and fell silent as he studied the names. Then, he started tapping the page.

"You recognize some of these surnames, don't you? Nelson, obviously. Then there's Campbell, which we don't know is related to Mayor Campbell. Hmph, if I were to venture a guess, I'd say that the survivors from this SJ squad hung around the area."

"Do you recognize any other names?" I asked.

Captain Nelson nodded. "Ryan Nelson, obviously. Then there's Darryl Jones. It's such a common surname that you never know who could be related. Henry Woodson and James Besch. Both names are familiar to anyone who knows the history of our town. Peter Quinn and Christian Campbell. Again, no promises, but I think those two could be related to the mayor and one of the councilmen."

Vance tapped my shoulder. "Do you realize how

many that leaves?"

"Six," I breathed. "I think we just identified the six who were found on my land: the remaining members."

"Any ideas what the causes of death were?" the captain inquired.

"The remains were stolen," Vance reported. "The only way we'll ever know is if they're recovered."

"In that case, they just became your top priority," Nelson said, wagging a finger at my friend. "PV will *not* be known as the town where gravediggers still roam, get my drift?"

"Loud and clear, sir."

"Good. That will be all."

Back in Vance's office, the two of us brainstormed scenarios that would meet the facts. Expulsion was first. Could the squad have been driven away from their base of operations? Then Vance suggested miscommunication. He thought maybe the squad relocated due to a misunderstanding with their HQ. That's about when I reminded my friend that several requests had been sent, asking to relocate to the PV area and all had been denied. So, my idea had been the squad took it upon themselves to relocate, fully expecting that their request would be approved. Maybe they never received the answer? Then again, there were multiple requests, so that meant they *knew* going to PV would violate their orders. That had to be out.

Vance finally brought up the uncomfortable topic: desertion. The most likely suggestion had simply been the men had wanted to relocate, and refused to take no for an answer. Therefore, they moved their squad anyway, regardless of consequences.

"What would entice enlisted men to abandon their posts?" Vance wondered, sitting back in his chair.

"You do realize what had started around ten years before the Civil War, don't you?"

Vance fixed me with a stare. "All right, Mr. PBS, let's hear it."

"Oh, come on. You've lived here longer than me. The beginning of the Oregon Gold Rush? Ring any bells?"

Vance whistled as he leaned forward to rest his elbows on his desk.

"My bad, pal. I had forgotten about that. So, your theory is that the temptation to dig for gold was too great, so they all deserted?"

"Not all of the 4th, but it sounds like everyone from this particular squad," I corrected.

"Then, what happened to them? Why did those six die under your house?"

"And on that note, I think it's time we head out."

Vance blinked a few times. "Huh?"

I tapped my watch.

"It's Friday afternoon. We're all due to meet at Casa de Joe's, remember? It's time to check out the corgi clues and see if we can—for once—figure out what these two have been trying to tell us before the case is solved."

Vance let out a short bark of laughter.

"Hah. Good luck with that one. We haven't been successful yet."

"They're dogs," I reminded my friend. "We've got to be able to figure this out before they do one of these times. That's not too much to ask, is it?"

"And you think that time will be tonight?" Vance scoffed.

I sighed. "Probably not."

* * *

Casa de Joe's seemed busier than normal. Practically every seat was taken, but thanks to me calling ahead and warning Joe, the owner, that a large party would be stopping by today, they were ready for us. Three tables had been pushed together, which allowed for a dozen people to join us. I personally didn't think we'd need that much room, but then again, the staff could always pull a table off should they need the room.

Jillian and I entered the restaurant and were immediately directed to our table. Looked like everyone was in the mood for Mexican food tonight, since we were the last to show up. Harrison Watt, PV's primary veterinarian, and my best friend from high school, was here with Julie, his wife. Vance and Tori were also here. Dottie also had an open invitation to help us decipher corgi clues, so she was also here.

I was also surprised to see Hannah Bloom, one of Jillian's good friends, here, with her son, Colin. I got along well with both of them, since we frequently hang out together. Colin and I share a love of retro video games, and I rather enjoy blowing the kid away in Donkey Kong, Dig Dug, Robotron, and a slew of others. Each time I saw him, Colin would challenge me to some obscure game, thinking I wouldn't have heard of it or have any experience playing. Curious to see what he was going to suggest this time, I gave him an expectant look and raised both eyebrows.

"So, what's it to be, sport? Think you've found a game I know nothing about?"

"You won't," Jillian said, smiling at the boy. She pointed at me. "You realize he's just a big kid at heart, don't you?"

Colin took several steps toward me and placed himself directly in my path. With arms folded across his chest, he made his challenge.

"Next time we meet? *Wizard of War*. I've been practicing."

"*Wizard of War*?" I repeated, looking surprised. "I'm afraid there's no such game, kiddo."

A triumphant look appeared on Colin's face.

"Hah! There is so! Oh, I'm gonna wipe the floor with you!"

I held up a finger and smiled as I watched the smirk melt off the kid's face.

"The game is actually called *Wizard of Wor*. There's an O in Wor, not an A. And, I've played it quite a bit. Challenge accepted, my young adversary."

"Awww, man!" Colin complained.

"Pull up a seat, guys," Vance invited. "We're all anxious to prove we're smarter than a couple of dogs."

"And what are you going to be feeling when it's proven we're not?" Jillian challenged.

"They're dogs," Harry said, taking a sip from his glass of water. "The odds aren't in their favor, man. I think we're due. Come on, bro. Whip out the phone. Let's take a gander!"

The waitress arrived. Julie held up her hands and patted the air, indicating we should put our conversation on hold. She then turned to the young girl. After our drink orders had been placed, and bowls of chips, salsa, and bean dip were handed out, we all settled down and took the next ten minutes to catch up with each other. I didn't pull out my phone until our orders were placed before us.

"All right," I announced, raising my voice, "shall we get this party started? Who's ready to play, Are You Smarter Than a Pair of Corgis?"

Colin was the only one who raised his hand.

"Put your hand down," his mother instructed, in a soft voice. "It was rhetorical."

"Why do you say that?" the boy whispered back.

"Because, no one is smarter than those dogs."

"Whatcha got for us, bro?" Harry asked.

I opened my photos app and navigated to the

beginning of this case's corgi clues.

"Alright, first up, we have pictures of ... okay, this would be the trunk that was found inside my house's old foundation. Following it, we have, let's see. One, two, three ... a total of eight pictures, all of the trunk, and the area it was found in. Let's pass that around, will you?"

Jillian gave me a patronizing smile and took my phone.

"Can I make this a little easier for you?"

"Uh, sure. What do you have in mind?"

My wife started tapping and sliding her finger on my phone's display.

"If we make a shared photo album, and then invite our friends to be able to view them, then they can use their own phones to be able to look at the pictures."

"But, I'd have to send the pictures to them," I protested.

Jillian shook her head. "Not this way, you wouldn't. Okay, I created a shared album, and now I'm adding pictures. Which ones, Zachary?"

Leaning over Jillian's shoulder, I pointed out which photographs should be included.

"Now, we tap the Share option, and I put in everyone's phone numbers, and we can ... wait. Is there anyone here who doesn't have a cell phone like this one? Do we all have the same model?"

Hannah held up her phone, which was an older flip phone. "I'm pretty sure I don't."

"You're sitting next to me, so you can share

mine," Jillian told her. "As for the rest of you, if there's someone I forgot, let me know."

A series of chimes, beeps, and chirps sounded from everyone present. Phones were pulled from purses and pockets. In just a few moments, practically everyone at the table was now looking at the first set of pictures I had taken, and they were using their own devices!

"One of these days, you're going to have to tell me how you did that," I said to Jillian, giving her hand a squeeze. "Every time I think I'm making steps toward understanding these blasted gizmos a bit better, you're always there to give me my reality check. What would I do without you? At any rate, thank you. You're right. This is so much easier."

"All right, pal," Vance said, as he stared at his phone. "Take us through them."

"Right. Okay, if you're all looking at this new album Jillian set up, the first eight pictures show the area inside the hollow foundation. You can see where everything was found, especially since I moved it all out."

"You did?" Harry asked, looking up. "Why? I thought you aren't supposed to touch anything 'til the cops get there."

"It wasn't a crime scene," I pointed out. "Well, I guess it could be, but I didn't know it at the time. I was just surprised, like everyone else, to learn part of the old house's foundation was hollow."

"Even more so to discover it had the remains of

six people," Vance added.

"Very true. Does anyone have any questions?"

"Did Sherlock and Watson zero in on anything?" Julie asked.

I thought back to my initial examination of the soldiers' encampment.

"As a matter of fact, Sherlock did. He couldn't quite reach inside, so instead, I picked him up so he could look in. For the record, he lost interest after I took these shots."

Heads were nodding.

"Good to know," Harry said. "Okay, bro, what's with this next one? Where were you?"

"We're up to the ninth photo," I announced. "To answer your question, Harry, this was taken inside Carnation Cottage. Umm, let me think. All right, it's coming back to me. I was working on the book and Sherlock woofed to get my attention. I didn't know what he wanted, but later on, believe it or not, I *did* figure out what had attracted his attention."

"I'm all ears," Vance said, as he squinted at his phone.

"Put your glasses on," I heard Tori whisper.

"With this crowd? Not on your life."

Deciding to help save Vance's dignity, I described what was in the picture, which earned me a grateful head nod from my detective friend.

"Do you see the television screen? It had the tail end of a pizza commercial on it. That's what Sherlock was trying to get me to see: pizzas."

"Pizzas?" Vance repeated, looking up. "That makes absolutely no sense."

"Mushrooms," I explained. "I think the dogs were trying to alert me to the fact that there were mushrooms on the pizza."

"That's a bit far-fetched," Vance decided. "Even for you and the dogs. What about the second?"

"What about it?" I asked, puzzled.

"It doesn't look like the pizza commercial," Harry pointed out, coming to Vance's aid.

"It doesn't? Well, I don't know what to you tell you about it. I must not have hit the button fast enough. It's whatever came on after the commercial."

The table fell silent as we all studied the picture.

"It's a political ad," Hannah said. "I've seen that one before. It's an ad for Joe Mezzano. I don't remember who—or what—he's running for, I'm afraid. He's someone local."

I nodded. "Got it. Thanks."

"Even I could see that," Vance chuckled. "Maybe you'd like to borrow my …?"

"Don't be rude," Tori scolded.

"All right, all right. Zack, I'm sorry."

"No worries," I told him, waving off his concerns. "Keep listening, and you'll see why. Those two pics—mushrooms. Everyone remember that. Moving on."

"Who's this?" Tori wanted to know.

"Let's see. I only took one picture of him, so how that's relevant, I'm not sure. Here we have a photo of Professor Houston. He's the one overseeing the excavation inside that corner of the foundation."

"He's cute," Julie decided.

"Excuse me?" Harry all but sputtered. "You can't say that! Do you know how many times I've said that about a cute chick, and you ... ow!"

All of us, including Colin, turned to Harry and gave him an incredulous look.

"What? What'd I say?"

"Nothing, yet," I said. "You might want to keep it that way."

"Listen to him," Julie urged.

"Any ideas why the dogs wanted me to take the professor's picture?"

"What can you tell us about him?" Tori wanted to know.

I shrugged. "Well, he's from the University of Oregon. He's an archaeologist, obviously. He's participated in several international digs. Umm, he's friendly and polite. That's about all I have."

I noticed Jillian staring at her phone. She had zoomed the picture in as much as it would go and was studying everything she could see.

"See anything?" I asked, hopeful for a positive answer.

"Not really. Just a couple of theories. I'll expand on them if they pan out. What's next?"

I re-awakened my phone and studied the next four pictures.

"All right, the next four? They're taken at Hidden Relic Antiques. I was looking around Burt's shop when Sherlock and Watson stopped at this glass display. Inside was an ornate plate."

"Looks like it's made of gold," Hannah said.

"It does, doesn't it?" Jillian said, nodding. A look of surprise fell across her features. She hastily swiped left. "Zachary? This picture of Professor Houston? Look what he has on his left wrist."

Collectively, all of us swiped left, to return to the previous photo.

"It's a watch."

"A *gold* watch," Jillian corrected.

I returned to the picture of the plate.

"The plate isn't quite solid gold," I announced. "There are other colors there."

"Gold watch, gold plate," Vance muttered. "It might be a connection. And the next two? Looks like a sheriff's badge."

Jillian straightened in her chair. I watched her tap and slide her finger along her phone's display as she searched for something online. After a few moments, her face lit up. She handed me her phone and pointed at the screen.

"Look. Check out what position Joe Mezzano is applying for. Sheriff! He's hoping to get reelected for Josephine County sheriff."

"Sheriff?" I repeated. "And Sherlock looked at that sheriff's badge in Burt Johnson's place, didn't he?"

"What does the sheriff department have to do with anything?" Harry asked, puzzled.

"We're not sure yet," I told him. "But, we do

know the dogs have been fixated on all things police."

Vance snapped his fingers. "That's true. Captain Nelson, squad cars, and so on."

"Right. Moving on, we're now looking at a bunch of books."

"Where?" I heard Colin whisper.

"Dottie's bookstore," Hannah answered.

"Actually, we're still in Burt's shop," I said. "I had forgotten about this one. Sherlock and Watson pulled me over to this case and wouldn't budge until I took a picture. So, what's so important about these pictures?"

"I see a connection," Tori announced.

We all turned to Vance's wife.

"You do?" I asked. "By all means, please share with the class."

"Gold," Tori said,

"No, those are books," I corrected.

"I can see they're books, silly," Tori said, offering me a smile. "Look at the titles. Several of them are about Oregon's history and, more specifically, its role in the discovery of gold."

They did? How did I miss that? Pulling out my own cell, I was in the process of enlarging the picture, so I could see it for myself, when Jillian handed me hers.

"She's right. Three of the books actually talk about the start of the Oregon State Gold Rush."

I started ticking off points on my fingers.

"Gold watch, gold plate, and books on the gold

rush," I said, rubbing my chin. "I'm thinking—just thinking!—that gold factors in somehow."

"It's not hard to figure out how," Vance said. "Look at those six poor souls whose remains were found in your house. Didn't you just tell me, earlier today, that the soldiers more than likely deserted their posts because the temptation of newly discovered gold was too much to ignore?"

"I did."

"All right!" Vance whooped. "We're making progress! What else do we got?"

"*Have*," Jillian corrected.

"*Have*," Tori echoed.

"Fine, fine. What else do we have?"

I looked at the next two pictures and nodded.

"See? Here's where the mushroom bit comes in. These next two? I'm pretty sure it was for the same pizza commercial. Sherlock and Watson wanted me to know we should be paying attention to mushrooms."

"I strongly doubt that, bro," Harry said. "It's a commercial. You have no idea if Sherlock wanted you to check out mushrooms."

"Just a moment," Tori said, laying her hand over her husband's. "Let's assume, for the sake of argument, that Zack is right, and the dogs wanted us to look into mushrooms. Why? Is there something I missed?"

Jillian came up with the answer.

"Slippery Jack!"

"The name of their squad?" I asked, turning to

look at my wife. "What about it?"

"None of us really knew what the relevance of that name was, right?"

"Sure."

A few taps on her screen brought up the answer.

"A slippery jack is a type of mushroom, Zachary!"

It felt like my mouth fell open. Looking at Vance, I could see he had the same expression. Slippery jack was a type of mushroom? Who knew? Sorry, that was a dumb question. Clearly, the answer to that was Sherlock and Watson. Again, I don't know how they did it.

"How many more are there?" Harry wanted to know.

"A few more," I said. "Not too many. Let's see. Yep, the next four happened at the police station."

"Captain Nelson," Vance said, nodding.

"But, they aren't all of him," I pointed out. "The first two are of the station itself. Then, we have two of the captain and one of his collection of Civil War memorabilia."

"What about the last one?" Vance asked. "Oh, I remember this. I got you to take a picture of Officer Jones."

"Why?" Harry asked.

"And that's why we're here," I said, grinning. "Let's recap. We have pictures of the Civil War stuff I found, mushrooms, gold, politicians, and a bunch of cops."

Jillian held up a hand. "Just a moment. We have

pictures of the trunk, mushrooms, sheriffs, gold, and quite a few police-themed ones. I think we can deduce a few of them."

"What's deduce?" I heard someone ask.

Hannah turned to her son. "It means *figure out*. Hush."

Jillian smiled at the youngster and continued on.

"The mushrooms--I would say that pertains to the name of the unit of soldiers found in Zachary's foundation. The gold--that one is easy. Why were the soldiers in the foundation to begin with? What would cause them to desert their posts? Well, in this case, I'd say it's gold."

"I think that's a solid deduction." Glancing around the table, I waited for any other theories. "No one? Okay, my dear, care to keep going?"

"I could, but that's all I have at the moment. I really don't have any idea why there are so many clues pointing at the police. I'm hoping Vance can answer that one."

All eyes turned to my detective friend, who had just taken a sip of his margarita.

"Don't look at me. I'm in the dark just as much as the rest of you."

"Come on, bro," Harry urged. "You're the cop. Got any ideas?"

"*Have*," Jillian corrected.

"*Have*," Tori said, in unison.

"The only thing I can think of isn't very becoming," Vance admitted.

"We're just brainstorming," I said to Vance. "Whatcha got?"

Harry pointed an accusatory finger at me.

"Why didn't you two correct him? *Whatcha got*? That was way worse than me."

"He spoke like that on purpose," Tori pointed out. "If he was trying to use that bad grammar in every day speaking, then I would have."

Jillian raised a hand. "Ditto."

"You guys suck."

Vance looked at me. "What about you, Zack?"

"I don't know," I admitted. "It feels like we're missing something."

"If you lost something, why don't you have Sherlock and Watson find it?" a timid voice asked.

We all turned to stare at Colin.

"What was that?" I asked. When it looked like the poor boy was about to collapse from nervousness, I took it upon myself to bring my fellow gamer out of his shell. "You said I should let Sherlock and Watson find something?"

Looking straight at me, Colin started to relax.

"Well, yeah. Your two dogs can find anything, can't they? Well, tell them to look for whatever you're looking for."

"I should do that," I chuckled.

"Have you let them look around?" Colin asked. "I mean, I know you don't live there at the moment. Let them out. See where they go."

"He's already done that," Vance said, as he nodded at the boy. "But, that's a really good idea,

Colin. I … Zack, what's the matter?"

"Have I?"

"Have you *what*?" Vance asked.

"Let them out. Let them look around my old house."

"Didn't you do that before?" Vance asked, frowning. "I swear you did."

"On leash, yeah. But, what if I do what Colin suggests. What if I let them off leash? What if there *is* something we're missing?"

The murmurings at the table stopped.

"Colin? I'm going to try your suggestion tomorrow. If this pans out, then I'm gonna buy you your own arcade machine."

Colin squealed with surprise and stared at me, open-mouthed.

"Maybe then, you'd be able to beat me."

The mouth snapped closed.

"Oh, it's on, old man. You won't know what hit you."

EIGHT

The following morning, Vance, my canine companions, and I were strolling along the grounds where my old house used to stand. Since Colin had suggested letting Sherlock and Watson search for clues, I had made the (probably foolish) comment that, should they find anything useful, that I'd personally buy the kid his own arcade machine.

So, here we were, letting the dogs search. Don't get me wrong, I would not want to foot the bill for yet another arcade machine, but I'm also a man of my word. Should either of the corgis find anything that the PV cops had missed when they were here, then Colin was going to get his chance to do some serious practicing. As soon as I unclipped their leashes, they took off. Many dog owners wouldn't do something like that with their dogs. By that, I mean unclipping them outside. My two dogs are corgis. They have yet to stray away from me whenever we're together.

"You know something?" I said, as the two of us idly followed the dogs across my property.

"What's that?" my detective friend asked.

"We never got around to talking about the Ireland sequel last night."

Vance shrugged. "Don't feel bad. I forgot all about it, too. So did Tori, for that matter. Tell me something, pal. Can you really pull this off? Do you think you can come up with some type of story that you can turn into a sequel?"

"And *that* was why I wanted some ideas," I said. I saw that Sherlock and Watson had suddenly changed course, and were now heading back to where the laboratory/tent had been set up. "I'm thinking maybe we can get a few ideas which might get ye olde creative juices flowing."

Vance gave me a despondent look.

"You have no idea what to write about, do you?"

Exasperated, I let out a sigh.

"There's a reason I wrote it as a standalone. I've tied up everything. There are no loose ends, there are no unresolved conflicts, and there are no villains plotting their revenge. In this case, the situation *was* the antagonist, and seeing how Tori's character made it through the famine with flying colors, I consider the story nicely wrapped up. No, if we're going to do a sequel, a new problem has to present itself, and what's more, there has to be an equal chance that our heroine will not be able to overcome it."

"I think I see where you're going with this,"

Vance said, as we continued to walk.

"Don't get me wrong, it's doable," I clarified, "but difficult. Jillian and Tori are both avid readers. I'm not sure about Julie. They're the ones we need to run ideas by, and they'll let us know if it's believable, and most importantly, if it's already been done."

"Like they've read that many books," Vance scoffed.

"Believe it," I told my friend. "Jillian is always reading. For that matter, I read every night on my iPad."

"Really? Don't you get enough of books, having written as many as you have?"

"Are you kidding?" I exclaimed, not bothering to hide the disbelief in my voice. "I read not only because I enjoy it, but I look for ideas; inspiration. There are many times I come across a scene and think to myself, I could do it better. And, if I did, then I'd do it *this* way."

"I guess that makes sense," Vance admitted. "What sort of time frame are we looking at?"

"To writing another? As long as it takes."

"No, I meant, is there a date and time your publisher is requiring a response from you about this?"

"Oh. No, no date or time. Actually, I think my publisher would personally take you out to dinner if we could come up with a good story for an Ireland sequel. My publisher made a ton of money off that book and they would certainly be open for a chance to do it again."

"So did we," Vance reminded me.

"True. The next time we're all together, I think …"

"You think what?" Vance asked, after I trailed off.

"I think I have to buy another arcade cabinet."

"What? What are you talking about?"

"Look at the dogs. Sherlock has picked up on something. So has Watson. Looks like we're headed over to where the tent used to be."

Vance was silent as he watched the two corgis guide me, like a pair of oxen pulling a plow, over to a patch of dirt that had been very effectively trampled by numerous people walking over it.

"There's nothing there," Vance finally said, after a minute or two had passed.

"That either of us can see," I added.

Sherlock chose what looked like a random spot and started digging. After a few moments, he stopped. A look of what I could only describe as disbelief appeared on his face. Slowly, he turned to Watson. The two corgis locked eyes for a few moments before Watson sniffed the ground and ambled off, chose a spot, and started digging.

"Awwoooo," Sherlock protested, using a low, throaty howl.

Watson looked up. She shook her head, looked once at me, and returned to her digging.

"Awwooowooo."

"Uh, oh," I whispered, as a smile appeared on my

face. "Sherlock just added a syllable."

"What does that mean?" Vance whispered back.

"I'm pretty sure it means he's getting annoyed. For once, it's not me. I think he wants Watson to dig in the same spot as he is."

"Awwooowooooooooooo."

"Well, that one was longer," I reported. "Sherlock, let it go, pal. She either can't hear you when she's digging, or, more likely, she hears you just fine and has no intentions whatsoever of moving. Either way, you'd better plan on tackling this one by yourself."

Sherlock snorted once, looked back at Watson, and then resumed digging.

"I swear, he'd better not find any more human remains," I grumbled, crossing my arms over my chest.

Sherlock went full prairie dog on me. He hunched his back, dug in his rear paws, and started digging as though he was a rescue dog searching for survivors in the aftermath of an avalanche.

"Did he find something?" Vance eagerly asked.

I pointed at the dog. "Well, maybe. I missed Sherlock's explanation of why he was digging there."

"Ha ha. Nobody likes a smart aleck."

Sensing movement, I glanced over at Watson. She had stopped to watch her packmate for a few moments. And, quite honestly, I thought she was going to move next to him before she resumed her digging, but I was wrong. The red and white corgi returned to her hole and her digging began anew. Within moments, both corgis were covered with a fine layer of dirt.

"You guys are getting so dirty," I moaned. "And, I'm pretty sure it rained last night. You know what this means, right? Right?"

Sherlock paused long enough to look back at me, woof once, and resume his work.

"Look on the bright side," Vance said. "We could be in Arizona."

"At this time of year? Hah. You wouldn't find me outside, thank you very much."

"What did you do for fun down there?" Vance asked, as together, we watched the dogs tear up the ground, albeit in different locations.

"Whatever included an air conditioner," I said, thinking back to all the summers I spent in the desert, land-locked state. "Look what I do for a living. I stay behind a computer and write. That doesn't require me to venture outside."

"But, you could, right?"

"I could what, keep writing? Outside? Sure, I guess. I wouldn't, though. For me, it's just like … well, eating outside. I've never been a fan."

"Bull. You eat outside here all the time."

"That's because it isn't over a hundred-twenty degrees," I reminded him. "Or, over a hundred in the shade. No, Samantha and I pretty much kept inside for the summer months. Granted, it wasn't always like that. The majority of the year was really pretty."

"But, you were still in the middle of a desert," Vance pointed out.

"True. What about here? Winters can stretch out over, what, six months? Seriously, it snowed in October, and snowed again in April."

"Okay, that's true," Vance had to admit, "but it doesn't happen all the time."

"You know what? I don't think I've ever asked you before. Were you born and raised in PV?"

Vance shook his head. "I'm afraid not. I was born and raised in Anaheim. Tori's family came from Cerritos."

"Why did you move here?"

Vance turned to me. "Didn't I ever tell you?"

"No."

"Tori wanted out of the big city. She wanted to start a family, and she didn't want to have to worry about crime striking too close to home. We used to take drives, every weekend. I remember taking weekend outings, just to check out the surrounding areas. I always thought it was because Tori wanted to get out of our little apartment. Little did I know she was scouting for a new place to live. Well, one day, we were driving through northern California and saw how close we were to the Oregon border. Figuring why not, we drove the extra forty-five minutes to reach Ashland and Medford. As we explored the area, we stumbled across PV, and the rest is history."

Movement in our peripheral vision had us both stopping. We turned to the dogs and watched as Sherlock stopped digging, gave himself a solid shake, and then turned to face me.

"What? What are you staring at me for? You're the one doing the digging."

"Not any more, he isn't," Vance helpfully supplied. "Sherlock, did you find what you were looking for?"

In response, my tri-colored boy dropped his nose and pawed at the dirt. Then, he scuffed the ground with one of his stumpy forelegs. Not finding anything to his liking, Sherlock resumed the position and just like that, clumps of damp soil, small pebbles, and a few weeds were flying through the air once more. For the record, Watson never stopped.

Several minutes later, at the exact same time, both corgis paused, lifted their noses as if someone had started barbecuing rib-eyes, and looked at each other. They both shook the excess dirt off their fur, walked over to my side, and promptly sat. Not sure what they were playing at, I quietly clipped their leashes back into place.

"What are they doing now?" Vance wanted to know.

"Beats me. Did they find what they were looking for?"

Vance wandered over to the newly formed dirt pile and nudged it a few times with the toe of his shoe. Then, he stopped, dropped to a squat, and fished something off the ground. Staring at the whatever-it-was in his hand, Vance fell silent as he apparently considered the ramifications of what he was holding.

"What do you have there?" I asked. "Curiosity kills, pal. Spill. What did Sherlock find?"

"I can see why Sherlock and Watson have become so intent on getting us to focus on the police," Vance said, using an eerily neutral voice. "Political ads, badges, and even the captain."

"Why?' I asked, growing anxious. "What'd you find?"

Vance held his hand out to me and waited for me to see for myself what had spooked him.

"I hate to state the obvious," I began, "but is that, or is that not, a button?"

"It's a button," my friend confirmed.

"And this concerns me *how*?" I asked.

"Zack, this is a button off of a Class B standard duty uniform. This means one of our officers lost a piece of their uniform, right here, on your property."

"That's not too surprising," I said. "We've had plenty of cops going through here. In fact, I've seen a few in the tent before. That is, when it was still here. What are you saying, Vance? That the police are somehow responsible for … for … the theft? After all, that's what the tent was primarily used for, analyzing anything unearthed from the foundation."

"*Woof.*"

Together, the two of us turned to look at Sherlock. My little boy had reared up on his hind legs, placed his filthy front paws on my knee, and was trying to get his snout as close as he could to the object Vance was holding. Seeing this, Vance squatted and held the button out. Sherlock was immediately there and nudged it, almost making Vance drop it.

"You don't get any clearer than that," my detective friend announced, rising to his feet. "Sherlock, Watson, You did great! Umm, Watson, you can stop digging now."

Watson was too busy having the time of her life. She was facing away from us and continuing to dig, prairie dog style. I stepped forward and gently touched her back. The dirt being flung between her hind legs instantly stopped. My red and white girl shook herself and turned around. She gazed proudly at the hole she had dug and rubbed against my leg. Reaching down, I gave her a thorough scratching behind her ears.

"Good job, girl. That's one heck of a hole. And look at the pile of dirt you created! Well done!"

Not to be outdone, Sherlock thrust himself forward, effectively pushing Watson out of the way so he could get his turn in the spotlight.

"Yes, Sherlock. You did a fantastic job, too. So, what now?"

Vance pulled out a small evidence baggie from one of his pockets.

"This goes into evidence. I doubt they'll be able to get anything off of it, but we could … do you hear that?"

"Do I hear *what*?" I asked, lowering my voice.

"I hear a car coming."

"It's bound to happen, buddy," I said, snickering. "It's quiet enough out here to be able to hear when a car is approaching."

"Woof!" Sherlock warned.

"Ooooo!" Watson agreed.

Apparently, we weren't the only ones who were interested in waiting for the oncoming car to appear. The dogs, though, had given off a warning woof. What did that mean?

An older orange and brown two-tone pickup truck appeared. It looked like it had seen its fair share of adventure; it was covered in small dents and scrapes. The truck slowed to a stop. Thinking the truck belonged to the neighbor, or else was simply visiting, I turned around and had already taken several steps away when I realized I hadn't heard any other sound from that pickup. I had assumed they were going to pull off at the neighbor's house just down the street. However, the truck remained motionless on the side of the road.

"Recognize him?" Vance asked.

"No. I thought it might be someone who wants to visit with my neighbors, but right now, I can't figure out what he's doing."

"All right, he's moving now," Vance reported, as he slowly walked along my driveway, headed to the street. That's when whomever was driving the truck gunned the motor, and spun the tires, effectively making the old truck do a half-donut. Once it was facing the opposite direction, it peeled out.

"Is that suspicious, or is it me?" I asked, as I turned to look at my friend. "Can you tell what make of truck it is? Surely, it isn't the same one that was here earlier, is it?"

Vance was staring at the dogs. Sherlock and Watson were practically jumping up and down, barking maniacally. My detective friend slowly turned to look in the direction the truck had gone.

"Zack, I think it's a Silverado, which makes it a …?"

"A Chevy!" I answered, growing excited. "Sherlock, Watson, want to go on a ride?"

Right on cue, both dogs stopped their barking. Sherlock let out an exasperated single bark and made for my Jeep.

"This way, boy," Vance called, as he hurried to his sedan, a 1980 Oldsmobile Delta 88. The diesel engine fired up and Vance gunned it a few times as I loaded the corgis in the back seat. Before placing the car in gear, my detective friend reached behind his seat, grabbed a vintage cherry light, and slapped it in place on his dashboard, and not on the car roof. "Plug that in, would you?"

"You've got to be kidding me," I snorted, as I took the old-fashioned DC cord and plugged it into the cigarette lighter. "I can't believe you still use this thing."

"You and everyone else. Hold on!"

The sedan tore down my driveway and skidded over the asphalt as we made a sharp right turn. Vance floored the accelerator as he pulled out his phone.

"Detective Vance Samuelson, in pursuit of a two-tone Chevrolet pickup truck. What's that, ma'am? Orange and brown. Suspect is sought in connection with the theft of excavated artifacts at Lentari Cellars. Yes, that robbery. No, it's not in sight yet. I'll give you details just as soon as I have ..."

"WOOF!" Sherlock exclaimed.

"I'm sorry, ma'am. Please hold the line. Zack, why is Sherlock barking? Does he see something?"

"The street you just passed ... He and Watson are both staring at it. I think the truck must've turned off this road!"

Vance tossed me the phone and then forcefully spun the wheel, directing the car to slide into a rapid U-turn and before I could mutter a choice profanity, we were rapidly heading toward the fork in the road. Turning left, Vance sped down the street, muttering softly under his breath.

"To think that a cop is responsible for this. A cop! When I get my hands on him—or her—I'm going to wring their neck! I ... what is it, Zack?"

"He's turned again," I said, looking at the dogs. "Sherlock and Watson are now looking at that small side road you passed."

"You could've said something sooner," Vance complained, as he brought the sedan to a screeching stop. Spinning the wheel, he reversed onto a person's driveway and then drove off, in the direction we had just come. "Which one? This one, on the left?"

I looked at Sherlock. Both corgis were looking left.

"Right."

"Right it is."

"No, I mean left!"

"You said right!"

"I was agreeing with you. Go left."

"Fine."

A few moments later, we got a very welcoming sight: the truck became visible in the distance. However, the driver must have caught sight of us, because we noticed a very visible increase in speed.

Vance held out a hand. "Phone!"

I slapped it into his palm, much like a nurse giving the doctor a scalpel when asked for it. While Vance radioed in our location, I turned to look at my dogs. Both Sherlock and Watson had their mouths open, their tongues hanging out, and were both drooling. Each was having the time of their lives.

"Backup is on the way," Vance reported, as he placed his cell in an empty cupholder on the arm rest. "I want to know who this turkey is, and how he's connected with the police. What was he doing sneaking up on us like that?"

"Based on *their* reactions," I began, "and assuming this person is somehow linked to the police, I'd say they were on their way to search for that button."

"I highly doubt that."

"Look at the facts!" I insisted. "I've been spending my time at Jillian's place while waiting for this investigation to wrap up. The dogs are obviously with me. We aren't supposed to be here, so unless Caden is out inspecting the fields, who would think twice if a cop stops by to check out the area?"

"You're forgetting a scenario," Vance said, as he continued to take us closer and closer to town. "He's the thief, he knows what he did is bad, so he wants to return the stolen loot. But, before he can, he sees us and panics."

I had to nod. It certainly *was* a plausible scenario.

"I haven't seen that particular truck before," Vance said. "We don't know it's a cop, or an off-duty one. But, before you say anything, I will admit that the facts seem to support your theory. I just want to see who's driving."

"You and me both."

We were nearing downtown PV, so the traffic started to pick up. The truck, unfortunately, was now weaving through the traffic as though we were on a four-lane freeway. The orange and brown pickup came dangerously close to clipping a small hybrid two-door as it darted around the slower-moving vehicle.

"The street is getting too busy," Vance

complained.

A siren sounded in the distance. Two patrol cars appeared behind us. Thanks to their sirens, the roads began to clear, only that meant the fleeing driver had plenty of room to floor his vehicle. Reaching speeds of nearly sixty—which didn't sound too bad until you realize the limit was twenty-five through the city, Vance held back.

"We're gonna have to call it. We can't let anyone get hurt."

"You mean we're going to let them go? Oh, man, this stinks."

"Life is too short, pal," Vance told me, as he unplugged his cherry light and pulled to the side of the road. Both squad cars did the same. "Captain Nelson has said, on more than one occasion, that a high-speed pursuit should *never* take place in the city."

I turned to the dogs, who were on their feet and quickly looking in all directions.

"We may not be done just yet. Vance, check out Sherlock and Watson. I think they know we lost them and they're now trying to figure out which way to go."

"What do you think, pal? Can Sherlock find the truck?"

"I don't know. Why don't you ask him?"

"Spoken like a true smartass. Zack, are you partial to splitting up?"

"Uh, sure, I guess. What do you have in mind?"

Vance rolled his window down and motioned

for one of the squad cars to pull up next to him.

"Franco! Would you take Zack and Watson in your car? I'll keep Sherlock with me. If we split up, then we can cover more area."

"You're inviting me to participate in an investigation?" Franco asked, perking up.

"Only if you stop asking me questions. The longer you stall, the farther away this guy will get from us."

"You got it, Detective. Mr. Anderson, come on over."

I looked at Sherlock.

"You're going to stay with Vance. Be a good boy, 'kay? Watson, you're with me. Come on."

Watson didn't need to be asked twice. She jumped into my arms even before I was ready to catch her. Thankfully, this is something both dogs do on a regular basis, so I was able to catch her without too much fuss. Carrying her to Officer Franco's car, I set her in the backseat and promptly took the front. Vance tore off, heading west on Main. Franco and I decided to reverse course and head back to town.

"How does this work?" Officer Franco wanted to know, after we were heading east. "Will Watson, er, tell you when we need to change direction?"

"You, too?" I asked, laughing. "What do you think she's going to do? Lean forward, tap us on the shoulder, and politely instruct us to take the next turn?"

Franco chuckled. "No, I guess not."

"What we're looking for is either a warning woof, which means she wants our attention, or if she is suddenly looking out the window. Otherwise, if nothing catches her fancy, she'll settle to the floor and fall asleep."

For close to thirty minutes, Officer Franco Trujillo and I patrolled all the main streets in Pomme Valley, and let's face it, there weren't many. After the third pass down Main, and up around Oregon Street, inspiration struck and I pointed west.

"Go that way, would you?"

"What for?" Franco asked.

"With as many people looking for this truck as there are, if he was in town, he would've been spotted by now."

"Think he made a run for Grants Pass?" Franco asked, as he turned his squad car right and we headed for the opposite side of town.

"Possible, but I don't think so. I personally think this guy has parked this truck somewhere and is currently hiding. We just have to find him."

We were both silent as we headed out of town. Signs started to appear, informing us we were approaching the junction of I-5. We were less than a mile from being able to merge onto the freeway when I noticed movement. Turning to look behind me, Watson had stirred, and was now sitting up, on her haunches. My little girl was ignoring me, and I could see she only had eyes for the passing scenery. Had she picked up on something?

"What's out this far?" I asked.

Franco shrugged. "Rupert's Gas & Auto is about the only thing out here before you hit the freeway."

"A gas station," I mused. Turning back to Watson, I saw that she was now fidgeting, as if she couldn't get comfortable. "Head for the station, would you?"

"You want to check out Rupert's? Sure. Here we go. They've got a few customers here, but I don't see the truck anywhere."

"Rawr wahr."

"What was that?" Franco asked. "Was that your stomach? At what point did we pick up Chewbacca?"

"Sure sounded like it, didn't it? Watson, I know that was you, but since when do you sound like that? You've never made *that* noise before."

Watson looked at me, opened her mouth, and panted. Then, she looked pointedly at the gas station.

"That's our cue," I said, growing excited. "Watson is picking up something at Rupert's."

"I'm calling it in," Franco said.

Vance's sedan pulled up at the same time. My friend rolled his window down and stared at us.

"What are you guys doing here?"

I pointed at Watson. "She just spoke Wookie."

"Watson spoke Wookie," Vance carefully repeated, with a grin on his face. "Does that mean what I think it means?"

"What are you doing here?" I asked. "Were you

following us?"

"I was following Sherlock's nose. He's the one who wanted to come here. I just followed the direction he kept looking. How long have you been here?"

"We pulled up a split second before you," Franco reported. "I'm surprised you didn't see us."

The five of us got out. Vance handed me Sherlock's leash. Then he nudged Franco and pointed in the opposite direction.

"I'll go this way, and you head that way. Let's see if this truck is parked somewhere nearby."

It wasn't. Ten minutes later, after doing a very thorough investigation of the area, both Officer Franco and Vance reported the same thing: no signs of an older Chevrolet pickup.

"Now what?" Vance wanted to know.

I felt several tugs on the leash. Looking down, both corgis were on their feet and pulling, wanting to head off in the direction Vance had gone, which was circling counter-clockwise around the station. Vance nodded and, together, we all followed the dogs as we moved past the service bays and rounded the backside of the station.

"There's nothing back here," I heard Franco tell Vance. "We've already checked it out."

"You're not them," Vance said, pointing at the dogs. "Until those two turn up nothing, I'm going under the assumption that *someone* is here. Maybe hiding? Who better to find a hiding person of interest than a couple of dogs?"

Wrong again. It wasn't a person. Sherlock and Watson pulled me up to the dumpster, which was the type that had two flaps acting as lids. Both lids were flipped closed, making certain a gust of wind wouldn't relocate any of the trash that had been deposited within.

"You searched the dumpster, didn't you?" Vance whispered to Franco.

"We were looking for a truck," Franco quietly answered. "And no, I'm not going in there unless I absolutely have to."

"Cover me. Zack? Stay back. Franco? Here we go."

Vance unholstered his weapon and at a sign from Officer Franco, flipped both lids back, opening the dumpster. Franco leapt forward, gripped the side of the dumpster, and thrust his gun inside.

"PVPD! Don't move! Hmm. Detective, you might want to see this."

"Who do you have?" Vance asked, hurrying over.

"It's not a who, but a *what*. What does that look like to you?"

Vance and I stepped up to the dumpster and peered inside. A grin appeared on my face and I let out a whoop. Turning to Watson, I gave her a hug. Inside was a very distinctive black container, with a bright yellow lid.

"Well done, girl! You found the stolen artifacts!"

NINE

T hat is such wonderful news!" Professor Houston was saying, over my cell phone's speaker. "I'm so relieved. The missing rifle. The sword. All the containers. They've all been recovered?"

"Well, not exactly," I amended. "There was one very noticeable absence: the bones. The container with the rifle and the sword was recovered, but it was the only one. The two with the bones in them haven't turned up yet."

Vance and I had carefully transferred the stolen container from the dumpster into the vehicle. I ended up opening the container so that I could see for myself what was inside. The rusted hilt from the cavalry sword was the first item to be discovered. I also saw several piles of decaying fabric. Shirts? I didn't know any had been stolen.

"Wait a moment," Professor Houston said. I could hear the surprise in his voice. "You recovered the rifle and the sword, but not the remains? Those weapons were *in* the box of remains. Well, one of them. That means someone would've had to open the transport containers, pull anything that wasn't human remains out, and then seal it back up? Where's the sense in that?"

"Someone is seriously motivated to keep those remains out of your hands," Vance said.

"But why?" I demanded. "The only thing we're planning on doing with them is to give them a proper burial. Or, at the very least, track down any living relatives and let them make that decision."

"No remains," Steve repeated. We all heard him sigh on the phone. "That's troublesome on so many levels. What I would like you to consider, Zack, is that … well, if those remains *are* recovered, I … *when*! I mean, *when* those containers are found, I'm truly hoping you'll consider letting us care for them. The knowledge we could glean from that collection of bones would be invaluable."

"Tell you what. If no one comes to claim them, they're all yours."

"You really think none of their families will take the bones?" Vance asked, leaning forward to place his face over the phone. "They're veterans, soldiers. They deserve a proper burial."

"Let's go with your plan, Zack," Professor Houston was saying. "Track down the descendants of those remains and see if they would like to handle the funeral arrangements. Then, and only then, if there are no takers, the museum will gladly take possession."

"You're on, pal."

"And the other items?" Steve asked.

"You mean the rifles, clothes, and personal effects?"

"Yes."

"I've promised a friend in town first dibs at them. He owns an antique store, and I know he's a history buff, too. Plus, I've had several friends step forward and openly request I give them a few pieces. The guns, for instance."

"What about the sword?" Professor Houston asked.

"That rusted sword? I may not like guns, but I've always been fond of swords. I was originally thinking about restoring the saber, but I think I'll settle with getting it cleaned up as much as possible."

"So, you're keeping it?"

"I hear the disappointment. Sorry, Doc. You're right. I'm keeping the sword."

Sherlock and Watson perked up. The corgis rose to their feet and immediately looked to the right. At that exact time, Captain Nelson appeared, distracted by a conversation with Officer Franco. After a few moments, he turned our way and saw the makeshift tables we had set up. His eyes widened with surprise as he peered inside the container.

"Mr. Anderson. Is it safe to say you've recovered the stolen artifacts? Oh, are you on the phone?"

I held up my cell, but indicated the intrusion

was welcome. "Yes, we've recovered some of the items, but no, it's not all of them."

"What's still missing?" the captain wanted to know.

"The bones," Vance reported. "All six individuals who had been recovered are still at large."

"Keep searching. I'm sure they're out there, somewhere."

"Do you think there might be anything left over that you'd be willing to donate to us?" the professor asked. Overhearing, Captain Nelson paused, and looked back at the table holding the recovered items. That's when I saw him linger for a few moments and, oddly enough, a flash of uncertainty appeared on his haggard features. Was it me, or did it look like the good captain was hiding something? "We would be delighted to accept whatever you see fit to throw our way."

"I've just never heard about anyone donating old bones," Vance said. "Isn't there some type of biohazard laws that prevent anyone from giving away DNA samples?"

"I'm sure there are some guidelines," the professor's voice confirmed, "but the ability to donate your body to science has been around for years."

"True. I hadn't thought about that."

Interest piqued, the captain reversed course and appeared at the table. "What's going on? Did I hear that right?"

"The University of Oregon has offered to take

the remains," I quietly explained.

"Is that so?"

Such was the tone that I felt the hairs on the back of my neck stand up. Was it me, or did the captain sound slightly annoyed? Again, I got the feeling that there was something he wasn't telling us. That's about when I felt a jab in my ribs. Vance was standing next to me, but he was staring at Captain Nelson. Based on the look on Vance's face, he clearly thought the captain was hiding something, too.

"It is, indeed," Professor Houston exclaimed. "You see, it's so very important to … just a moment. Who am I addressing? I know Zack's voice, and Detective Samuelson's."

"This is Captain Nelson, of the Pomme Valley Police Department."

"Ah. Good day to you, Captain."

"Thanks. What were you saying about wanting the remains found at Mr. Anderson's winery?"

"These are the remains of actual Union soldiers," the professor explained, slipping into the lecture voice I've heard him use a few times. "They had families, and they more than likely have extended family members alive today. We owe it to them to treat the remains with respect. But, if we're unable to find anyone who's willing to take the bones, then the museum will step up and see to it they're treated properly. Zack, I just thought of something. Did you say there was a personal Bible among the collection of effects?"

"That's right. You didn't see it in that crate because Burt is trying to locate that soldier's family. Phooey. I can't remember the name of the soldier. What about it?"

"Those are the types of items the museum would love to have in its collection," the professor told me.

"You'll have to take it up with Burt. Perhaps the museum would be willing to purchase the items from him?"

"There is that," Professor Houston admitted. "Could you text me his store's name and number? I'll call him myself."

"You got it, pal."

After the call had terminated, I was surprised to see that the captain was still standing nearby. He was staring down at the recovered rifle, which had been placed on a folding table set up for this purpose. Figuring he might be wondering if this was the rifle I was going to give him, I tapped his shoulder.

"Just to let you know, the one that was stolen, which was this one, is going to Vance."

A smile briefly appeared on Captain Nelson's face.

"You're a good man, Mr. Anderson."

Figuring that was the end of the conversation, I turned away, but noticed the dogs were still staring at him. Confused, I turned back. There was the captain, still standing motionless next to one of the open crates of recovered items.

"Is everything all right?" I quietly asked.

"Is there any way I could take a look at the cavalry sword that was found?"

"Sure. Vance, want to give me a hand? Could you grab the sword?"

The cavalry sword was actually on the table, but on the other side of the open container, which explained why the captain didn't see it.

"Here it is. Just a second. Something tells me I should be wearing gloves. There we go. Captain? If you'd care to put on a pair, I'm sure Zack will let you hold it."

"Look at the pommel cap, would you? Tell me if you see anything."

Vance held the sword out to me. "Here. He wants you to look at the pommel cap. For the record, what is a pommel cap?"

I tapped the butt of the sword hilt. "It's right here. Hang on, it's kinda dirty. Yeah, I can see something. Umm, it looks like letters."

"An RN?" Captain Nelson asked, with a heavy sigh.

"The first letter is definitely an R. The second? Hmm. It's kinda hard to tell. Looks a little like an O. Hold on. I think it all depends on how the letters were drawn. If it wasn't capitalized, or else the style of writing is different … yeah, that could certainly be an N. Wait. RN? Wouldn't that mean …?"

"You have no idea the amount of stress and anxiety your discovery has caused me," the captain said, lowering his voice to a whisper. "I knew this would see the light someday. I never thought it'd be with you, Mr. Anderson."

Overhearing, but situated behind the captain, Vance looked at me with a questioning look. I gave a very slight shake of my head. Vance nodded and immediately returned to his office.

"What's the matter, sir?" I asked.

"This is not news, Mr. Anderson," Captain Nelson said, "and shouldn't come as a surprise to you."

"The only guess I can come up with is that Ryan Nelson, er, Private Ryan Nelson, is your ancestor."

Captain Nelson nodded. "You will recall, I already told you my great-great-grandfather was in the Civil War."

Nodding, I flashed the captain a smile. "Hey, there's nothing wrong with that. I'm seriously thinking about doing research on my own ... what's the matter? Was it something I said?"

"And Ryan Nelson wasn't a private, but a sergeant."

"Umm, all right. That just means ... wait. How do you know that?"

"Come with me," the captain quietly instructed.

I was about to give the leashes a soft tug, to get the dogs' attention, but then noticed I didn't have to worry. Both Sherlock and Watson were on their feet and already following the captain out the door. In complete silence, we made our way to his office. Once inside, he closed the door, then reached for the shadow box with his collection of patches and other various bits of Civil War regalia.

Working in complete silence, Captain Nelson carefully opened the box, but not before snapping on his own pair of latex gloves. Fully protected, he reached inside and started removing the various pieces, one at a time. Setting them reverently on his desk, he kept at it until everything had been removed from the box. Unwilling to look my way, or meet my eyes, he reached in a final time and gently pressed down on the felt backing. Much to my surprise, two small indentations, located close together, appeared. Slipping the tips of his fingers into the indentations, the captain pinched them together, allowing him to remove what was clearly a false backing to the box.

Curiosity drove me forward, intent on seeing what had been revealed. With the removal of the false wall, I could see that the depth of the box increased by about an inch, which allowed for something to be concealed. In this case, I could see a small, leather book. It looked old.

Captain Nelson gingerly picked up the book and set it on his desk. I stood next to him and, together, we studied the leather tome. I figured it must have originally been dark brown or black but was now faded in several places. The leather was noticeably worn, and the corners and spine showed signs of cracking. The leather on the front cover was extended, to form a flap, and this flap was inserted through a slit in order to keep the book closed.

"That," the captain reverently began, "is the personal diary of Sgt. Ryan Nelson. In it, he ..."

Confused, and not sure I heard that right, I held up a hand, which brought Captain Nelson to an awkward silence.

"Yes?"

"Sir, if you're going to tell me what I think you're going to tell me, and that book details the account of those men who lost their lives in the foundation of my old house, then it calls into question why you're making this known now. Did you not want anyone to know about it?"

"It's not exactly my family's shining moment, is it?" the captain returned. "As such, it's not something I typically bring up during a day-to-day conversation."

I pointed at the diary. "Are you telling me that everything we need to know about those men is in that book? What happened, what they're doing there, and what drove them to desert their unit?"

"And that's the magic word right there," Captain Nelson crossly muttered. "Deserted. For nothing more than a few gold nuggets."

"You've read this thing, haven't you?" I accused.

"I have, yes."

"Umm, sir, doesn't this give you motive to keep everything quiet?"

Captain Nelson gave me a blank look. Uh, oh. Had I just crossed a line?

"It would certainly look that way to an outside observer, wouldn't it? Hmm." He leaned over his desk and punched a button on his phone. A split second later, we could hear a soft ringing.

"Samuelson."

"Detective? Would you come to my office?"

"On my way, sir."

"What are you doing?" I quietly asked.

"You bring up a very fine point. To answer your question, yes, I know very well how this makes me look. So, to put those fears to rest, I'm removing myself from this particular case *and* revealing the existence of this diary, which, I'm ashamed to say, I should have revealed the moment all of this was uncovered."

There was a tap on the door.

"Come in."

"Captain?" Vance asked, poking his head in. "Did you need something from me?"

In response, Captain Nelson turned to me, nodded once, and promptly sat in his chair, behind his desk.

"There's something you need to know, Detective."

"Oh? What's that, sir?"

"I know full well which of the six members of the SJ squad had their remains stolen."

"You do? How's that, sir?"

"It's in there," I guessed, pointing at the faded leather book.

"What's going on?" Vance asked, growing suspicious.

"Remember when we wondered if Private Ryan

Nelson might be related to the captain?" I asked. "Well, long story short, he is. In fact, Ryan Nelson was not a private, but a sergeant. Let me guess. He was the one responsible for bringing the men from Grants Pass to PV?"

The captain nodded.

"And," I continued, "he was probably embarrassed about his role in his company's desertion, so he traded ranks with someone else."

The captain nodded again. Vance raised his hands.

"Wait a minute. What *is* that book?"

"The personal diary of Sgt. Ryan Nelson, of SJ squad," I answered.

"And we're just learning about this now?" Vance demanded, growing angry. That was about the time he remembered who was sitting on the other side of the desk. "Oh, I'm sorry, Captain. I shouldn't have shot my mouth off like that."

"No apologies necessary," the captain returned. "That's why we're all here. It was bothering me that you and your consultant had questions about everything found on Lentari Cellars property. Even more so because I had the answers. As I was telling Mr. Anderson earlier, this is my family's deepest, darkest secret. My ancestor was a deserter, and yet he helped found the town we all live in. Take a seat. I'll tell you everything you need to know about those men."

Vance fidgeted from foot to foot.

"I hate to ask this, sir, but it has to be done. Are

you responsible for the theft of the remains?"

"I am not," Captain Nelson declared. His eyes dared my detective friend to challenge his answer. Thankfully, Vance didn't press the subject.

"I didn't figure you did," Vance said. "That book? It tells why the men chose that particular spot for their camp and their hideout?"

"It's where they settled," the captain said, shrugging. "At the time, it was nothing but open grassland, with several hills here and there. They figured it was the perfect spot to try their luck as prospectors."

Vance pulled his notebook out and started scribbling notes.

"Were any claims made?"

"No. At least, not that Ryan mentioned."

"That's good to know," I said, chuckling nervously. "If a claim would have been made on land that I own, well, I think that means I'd soon learn that I wouldn't own nearly as much land as I currently do."

"Did any of them strike it rich?" Vance asked.

"Their remains were found in an old building's foundation," Captain Nelson reminded us. "I think it's safe to say that none of them became millionaires."

"Did it say when they deserted their posts?" Vance wanted to know.

"Yes. I know the answer to this. Let me think. I know the California Gold Rush started in the late 1840s. I found several passages claiming that mines were starting to dry up in California, so the miners were expanding outward. In 1852, gold was discovered right here in Pomme Valley. You should know, Mr. Anderson."

The question was all because I had a hand in the recovery, and the return, of a lost gold mine. And, the captain was right. It was there, in PV, just waiting to be discovered.

"I do, indeed," I announced, eliciting a grin from Vance.

"In April of 1861, the Civil War started," Captain Nelson stated, sounding like a very gruff, no-nonsense lecturer. "But, as you can imagine, in the great state of Oregon, or as it was known back then, the Oregon Territory, there wasn't a lot of action between the Union Army and the Confederates."

Sherlock and Watson slumped to the floor. Not out of boredom, but instead, wanting to get into a more comfortable position. Not to be outdone, I pulled out the closest chair and sat, prompting Vance to do the same.

"So, with no skirmishes with the Confederates anywhere in the territory, what do you think the men were responsible for doing?"

Captain Nelson paused, as if expecting one of us to answer.

"Don't look at me," Vance warned. "History is not one of my strong suits. Now, if you want to know about jazz, then I'm your man."

"Mr. Anderson?" the captain prompted.

"Indian raids and clashes among miners."

"Very good."

"Show off," Vance grumbled. "How did you know that?"

"Easy. I looked it up several days ago."

"Cheater."

"The life of a soldier in the nineteenth century was not an easy one, nor was it very rewarding," the captain explained. "So, I can only assume when local prospectors continued to strike it big, the temptation to claim some gold for themselves became too strong. Sgt. Nelson's squad deserted, at the recommendation of none other than my own ancestor. But, when they didn't strike gold, and it became apparent that they had made a huge mistake, they knew they were in trouble. The Army was not known for looking upon deserters with any type of favor. Deserters were known to be reassigned to work camps. Sometimes they'd be reenlisted for several more years. Did you know, that executions during the Civil War outnumbered those in all other American wars?"

"I did not," I confirmed.

"That makes two of us," Vance added.

"Turns out that many of the young men who enlisted had families in their care. What better way to provide for them than by serving in the military?"

"That couldn't have been an easy decision," I said, more to myself than anyone.

"A soldier's life isn't for everyone," Vance said.

"Especially during the war," Captain Nelson added.

"I get it. You're talking about land grants. The soldiers were given their own chunk of land as an incentive for enlisting. Why are you smiling, sir?"

Captain Nelson shrugged. "It's not often I get to correct you, Mr. Anderson. Him, I do it all the time. But with you, not so much. There were no land grants given during the Civil War. Soldiers could, however, deduct the time they served against the five year homesteading requirement."

"I did not know that, either. Thanks, Captain."

The head of PV's police force inclined his head toward the leather journal.

"That first-hand account of everything that transpired is irrefutable proof that nothing went according to their plan. SJ squad faced hardship after hardship, and when it became apparent gold wasn't going to be in their future, they resorted to living off the land. What was abundant in those parts?"

"Not gold," I guessed.

"Correct. Detective Samuelson, any guesses?"

"None, sir."

"Mushrooms. Those poor men lived off of mushrooms."

"Blech," I said, making a face. "I would have never survived back then."

"Oh, there's nothing wrong with mushrooms," Vance chided. "Especially if you cook 'em right."

"Why else do you think their squad was called

the SJs?"

"Oh, I thought that had been decided long before having to depend on mushrooms to keep you alive."

"How many times have you read that journal?" I wanted to know.

"Dozens and dozens of times," the captain answered.

I started picking off points on my fingers. "Starving, hiding from the army, trying to strike it rich, and let's not forget the many Indian raids that were happening on an increasingly frequent basis. I can't begin to imagine what they were going through. Having to deal with all of that *and* not finding anything worthy. Hey, I have a question. Did Ryan ever mention seeing any of the army patrols?"

"Yes, on more than one occasion."

"What about the house?" Vance asked. "Was there any type of structure located where Zack's future house was going to be built? By that, I guess I'm asking ... did the soldiers build some type of house right then and there? Or did someone come upon the site later and build something around them? What about Private Nelson? Er, Sgt. Nelson? He was a survivor, wasn't he? Could he have been the one to first build something on that land?"

A pensive look washed over the captain's features. He snapped on a fresh pair of latex gloves. He slid the diary over, opened the book to a page near the end, and started skimming. After a few moments, he let out a grunt, and gently tapped the page.

"Should've thought to look that up sooner. At any rate, yes, there was something there: an abandoned barn."

"The perfect hiding spot," I said, nodding.

"So, what killed them?" Vance asked. "And who was the one who sealed them into a building?"

"I've been asking myself that question over and over," the captain said, as he gently flipped to the last page in the journal. It was empty. "He didn't say."

"What *does* the last page say?" I asked.

Captain Nelson flipped the pages in reverse until the sergeant's scratchy scribbling was revealed.

"The only thing it says here is that Ryan Nelson returned to the barn a few days after venturing into town, to get supplies. When he returned, it was to a scene of carnage. Everyone in SJ squad was dead on the ground. What he described wasn't pretty."

"Dead?" Vance repeated, sitting forward.

"As a doornail," the captain confirmed.

"Someone poisoned them," I whispered.

Captain Nelson grunted once. "And *that* is precisely why I have never disclosed that I have this journal. I can't rule out that my own ancestor poisoned his men."

"But why?" I asked. "Why would he do that to his own men? Is there any mention of him striking it rich?"

"Not that I can find."

"What about dissention in the ranks?" Vance asked. "Maybe the men were planning a mutiny, and perhaps this Ryan fellow struck first instead of waiting for them to make the first move?"

Captain Nelson pointed at the journal. "If there was, then it'd be listed in there, and there's no mention of anything like it."

A notion occurred. Maybe it was because that's how active an imagination I had, or perhaps I really *did* watch too many movies. Another explanation loomed, and based on Sherlock and Watson's numerous clues, it fit in beautifully with what we knew about this case.

"What is it?" Vance wanted to know. "You're smiling. And, to top it all off, Sherlock and Watson are now staring at you, as though you just swiped the last doggie biscuit."

I looked at the journal. "That entire thing is written by Sgt. Nelson, right?"

The captain nodded. "Correct. What of it, Mr. Anderson?"

"I think there's another possibility we need to consider."

"And that would be?" Vance pressed.

"That our original assumption is incorrect. From the moment we learned the identities of the men in that encampment, we've been assuming something that, just now, I'm realizing, was completely false. There wasn't just one survivor, but two!"

TEN

So, we have a second survivor," Vance was saying. "That helps us *how*? I'm more interested in the current whereabouts of those bones, and who took 'em in the first place."

I turned to the captain, but he was just as lost as we were. All he could do was shrug. Vance then pointed at me.

"I think, for the first time ever, we need to revisit the corgi clues. We may have got a few things wrong."

"How is that going to help us?" I wanted to know. "We've been through them. I doubt they'll be able to tell us anything new."

Captain Nelson gestured for me and Vance to take a seat.

"I hope you two will forgive my curiosity, but I have heard about these clues your dogs have unearthed. If you don't mind, I'd like to sit in on this one. Besides, the human remains still haven't been recovered, and that's something I don't take very lightly."

Vance looked up, surprised.

"You want to watch us go through the pictures Zack has taken?"

"Afraid of being shown up by your boss?" the captain inquired, as a sly smile appeared on his face.

In response, Vance scooted his chair as close to the captain's desk as possible. I did the same. Both dogs, I should add, sank into down positions and looked as though they were moments away from snoring.

"To give you an idea how this works," I began, "when working a case, and the dogs zero in on something, I'll typically have no idea what they've found, so the best I can do is take a picture, which will then be viewed—collectively—with our friends at some restaurant."

"And one of you will be able to tell what the dogs are wanting to show you?" Captain Nelson asked.

"Oh, man, I would love to be able to tell you that we're experts in deciphering the whims of the corgis, but no. Not once have we figured it out before them. I honestly don't think it works that way. The clues Sherlock and Watson find will generally point us in the direction we need to go."

"I think I've got it. You may proceed, Mr. Anderson."

"Roger that. Now, both Vance and I have seen these pictures before, so we'll let you go first."

"Thank you. All right, what is this? It looks like

the insides of … oh, I get it. This is where the stuff was found? This is your property, Mr. Anderson?"

"Yes. Feel free to swipe through them. Like I said, we've seen them before."

We spent the next thirty minutes in silence. The captain slowly—and methodically—studied each picture. I watched the experienced police officer zoom in on various details. Keeping an eye on which picture he was looking at, I borrowed Vance's notebook and jotted down what we thought the dogs wanted us to notice: various police references, the picture of Professor Houston, which now that I'm looking at it, was showing the professor wearing a very gaudy golden chain around his neck.

I scribbled *gold* in the notebook.

Gold plates, sheriff badges, the pizza commercials … they all made it into the notebook. Coming across a photo of himself, I saw Captain Nelson blink with surprise. But, just like the other photographs, he studied every minute detail. Then, he did the same for his shadow box. Finally, the last picture appeared, and this one elicited a grunt of surprise.

It was of Officer Jones.

Handing me my phone, the captain leaned back in his chair.

"How would you have proceeded after viewing all of that?"

I presented my notes.

"We look for similarities. We try to find

meaning in the pictures. Why did I take a picture of traffic? What's so special about this rack of books in A Lazy Afternoon?"

"I get it. I don't say this often enough, but I'm impressed, Mr. Anderson."

Risking a quick look at Vance, I saw that my detective friend had rolled his eyes, but not before giving me a lopsided grin.

"Look at what I wrote here. As far as we can tell, we should be looking at the police, gold, antique police equipment, books about gold, mushrooms, and a slew of pictures of this station and you, of course."

"Mushrooms?" Captain Nelson said, frowning. "How did I miss that?"

"Pizza commercials," Vance said, grinning. "I know, right? It threw me for a loop, too."

Incredulous, the captain turned to look at me. "Is he serious? How did you make a mushroom connection from a pizza commercial?"

"Only that we could make out there were mushrooms on the pizza," I explained.

"All right, what about the picture of the bookcase?" Captain Nelson demanded.

"Taken from Dottie's store," I recalled. "Granted, there could be a more logical explanation, but I figure it had something to do with gold, or else it was about the discovery of gold in our area."

"Absolutely marvelous," the captain was saying. "And this second survivor? Do you know who it is?"

I looked at Vance. "Do you still have that list of everyone who was in the SJ squad?"

Vance took back his notebook and flipped a few pages.

"Yeah, I think so. I... here we go. Do you want me to list them all or should I just pick a few?"

"Read the names who sound familiar," I instructed.

"Pvt. Ryan Nelson, which we now know held the rank of sergeant. Then we have Pvt. Henry Woodson, Pvt. James Besch, Pvt. Peter Quinn, and Pvt. Christian Campbell, and finally, Pvt. Darryl Jones."

"Woodson could be a link to Spencer Woodson, from Toy Closet," I said. "Then again, Woody is one of the nicest guys I think I have ever met, so I don't think it's him."

Captain Nelson nodded. "Agreed."

"We have Pvt. James Besch," Vance continued, "who just so happens to share his last name with one of the most prominent primary care physicians here in town. Unless we're able to talk to each of them, to see if they're related, or else lived their whole life in town, I don't think we're going to know if we have a link."

"What do you suggest?" Vance asked.

I pointed at the dogs. "Something tells me we're going to know it when we see it. Or hear it. As is usually the case with these two, we're going to know the moment the link is revealed."

"Moving on," the captain said. "What are the

other names?"

"Campbell," Vance reported. "Pvt. Christian Campbell. What do you think? Any relation to the mayor?"

Had Mayor Debra Campbell lived in town her entire life? Did she have roots extending back over a hundred years? Possible, but unlikely. Besides, there was no way I was going to believe the mayor could be implicated in the theft of human remains.

"Who's left?" I asked.

Vance read the name in his notebook and looked up at me, eyes open wide.

"What is it?" I asked.

"Pvt. Darryl Jones."

"Jones?" I repeated, looking at the captain. "It's a common name, so I don't ... captain? What is it?"

"May I see your phone again?"

"Uhh, sure. Here you are."

Captain Nelson squinted at my phone and promptly handed it back.

"Bring up the pictures again, would you?"

"Sure. Here."

Vance and I watched as the captain swiped his way through the photos I had taken when he suddenly stopped. Holding my phone up, where we could each see it, the captain gave us a rare smile.

"What can you tell me about this picture?"

On the display, I could see a shot of a very familiar policeman.

"That picture ... let me think."

"I can tell you why he took that picture," Vance said. He tapped his own chest. "I asked him to take it. That shot was taken out at Lentari Cellars. Sherlock and Watson had started paying attention to the big tent, where the archaeologist and his students were storing everything they dug up. Officer Jones was there, looking through the tent. I chalked it up as professional interest. Then, I noticed Jones head toward the university's van. The dogs still hadn't broken eye contact, so I got Zack to take a picture."

"And once you did?" the captain asked, turning to me.

"Like with every other clue, once the photo was taken, the dogs lost interest."

"Absolutely fascinating. Samuelson, what can you tell me about Jones' behavior recently?

"Well, he always has a cheerful disposition. I've never heard Franco, his partner, ever speak a negative word about him."

"Send him in here, would you?" the captain requested.

Vance nodded and left the office.

"He has a common last name," I said. "It's just a coincidence."

"Let's hope so," the captain grumbled. "The last thing I need right now is to learn that one of our own was responsible for this theft. That's publicity I certainly don't need."

Vance poked his head back in the office, a look of alarm on his face.

"Uh, Captain? Franco says Jones hasn't reported in for duty yet. He was due nearly fifteen minutes ago."

"Does he drive an old Chevy truck?" I groaned.

Vance let out a nervous laugh, but sobered the moment Captain Nelson's eyes met his.

"I'll go find out," my detective friend said, hurrying off.

"There's no way it's him," I insisted. "I'd like to think a truck like that would have been noticed."

"A truck like *what*?"

"Well, it's an older Chevy pickup, with a two-tone color scheme: orange and brown."

Captain Nelson nodded. "You're right. We would have noticed something like that."

"He drives a newer Prius," Vance reported, as he appeared in the doorway. "There's no way it could be mistaken for that truck we saw."

"Well, so much for that option," I grumbled.

"*WOOF.*"

The three of us inside the office looked down at the dogs. Sherlock was on his feet and he was staring directly at the captain.

"Not this again. Look, you little fluffball. I had nothing to do with this. Yes, I guess in a convoluted type of way you could say I withheld evidence, but I had nothing to do with the theft. Can we leave it at that?"

"*WOOF.*"

"What's he doing?" the captain asked me. "What does he want?"

"If you didn't do anything, then there must be something you *can* do," I said.

"Or, something you know," Vance added.

Captain Nelson looked at the dogs and spread his hands. "I got nuthin', guys. The only thing I was thinking about suggesting was …"

Noting the sentence hadn't been completed, both Vance and I looked up.

"What was that, Captain?" Vance prodded. "You kinda trailed off, or else lost your concentration."

"Detective, check to see what family Jonesy has in town, would you? And … find out what they drive."

Surprised, Vance's eyebrows shot up. He nodded once and quickly left.

"You were *thinking* about family in the area?" I asked the captain. "Did I hear that right?"

"I was, yes."

I looked down at Sherlock. "Do we need to add telepathy to your list of skills? How did you know, you furry little booger?"

Sherlock's tongue flopped out and he panted. Whenever he did that, I couldn't help but think the look on his face had a smirk to it. I noticed Watson watching me and was about to ask her a question when she flopped over, exposing her belly. Chuckling to myself, I gave her stomach a few pats before remembering the captain was in the room with me.

"Dogs. I'll never figure them out. Especially these two."

"You clearly aren't meant to, Mr. Anderson. Well, here comes Samuelson. From the look on his face, I think he has some news."

"How did you know, sir?" Vance asked, the moment he joined us. "The only family Jones has in town is his father, who just so happens to live with him. The father has one registered vehicle in his name: a 1981 Chevrolet Silverado. Color—orange and brown. Captain, do you know what this means? One of our own has ..."

"That'll be quite enough," the captain said, lowering his voice to practically a whisper. "The last thing I want known is that one of our own people has become involved. We will deal with this internally; do I make myself clear?"

"Completely, Captain," Vance said, nodding. "How do you want to proceed?"

He rose to his feet and indicated Vance should follow. "We'll have a quiet powwow right now. Get everyone together, would you?"

"I'm on it."

"Mr. Anderson?"

Since I hadn't been invited to this hush-hush meeting among the police officers, and then again, why would I when I am, in fact, *not* an officer, I had remained seated inside the captain's office.

"Yes?"

"I'm going to need you and your assistants most of all. Be ready. We're going to find our missing man, get my drift?"

"Completely. I ... Captain?"

"Yes?"

"Look at those two. Something has them spooked. Or interested, but in what?"

My two corgis were practically pulling me off balance in an attempt to get out of the small office. Catching sight of my dogs, Captain Nelson stared a few moments before turning to look in the direction the dogs were angling toward. A split second later, a very unprofessional word echoed noisily around the busy room, bringing everyone to an uncomfortable stop in their activities. Vance was doing an admirable job of not snickering.

"Captain? Is everything okay?"

"Take a look at who just waltzed through the front door."

The entire room, myself included, turned to watch Officer Rich Jones come strolling into the station, as though he didn't have a care in the world. He saw the captain giving him an unreadable look, and then made eye contact with Vance, giving him an almost imperceptible nod. Sherlock chose that time to give himself a thorough shaking, which caused Jones to look his way. He briefly locked eyes with me before hurriedly looking away.

That one admission of guilt was all that was needed to convince me our prime suspect was clearly not the sharpest tool in the shed.

"Officer Jones," Captain Nelson. "Good of you to join us today. You're late."

"Oh, am I? I apologize, Captain. I lost track of the

time."

"My office, Jonesy."

"Yes, sir."

"Detective … Mr. Anderson. Join us."

Thankfully, the captain's office was bigger than Vance's, or else there wouldn't be room to breathe. Taking a seat, even before he was asked, was a bit tacky, if you ask me, but that's exactly what Officer Jones did. But, I will say this about our suspect. He was doing an admirable job of appearing unconcerned. Did he really think he had covered his bases that well?

"What can I do for you, Captain?"

"Oh, in a nutshell, you can tell us what you did with the human remains you stole from Mr. Anderson's property."

I was studying the officer's face intently, looking for tells. Jones blinked once, which told me he had already prepared a rebuttal. Crossing my arms, I leaned against the closed office door. The captain noticed my stance and pointed at me.

"See that? Mr. Anderson believes you just as much as I do. But, let's put that aside for now. Would you care to tell me where you were?"

"I overslept, Captain. It won't happen again."

"Overslept? It's two in the afternoon!"

"I, er, had a late night."

The captain grunted. "I'll bet you did. Well, let's start with … your uniform. Care to tell me why it looks dusty?"

Jones looked down at his shirt. "Dusty? I wasn't

aware, Captain. I'll make sure it gets cleaned."

"You'd think you hadn't worn that particular uniform in a while," Captain Nelson said, as he continued to exude an air of ambiguity.

Officer Jones brushed at a few pieces of imaginary lint on his chest. "I don't know about that, sir."

"Missing a button on your other uniform?" Vance asked, keeping his voice casual.

Jones blinked again, this time with surprise evident on his face. "Huh? I … I don't follow you, Detective."

"Mm-hmm. Well, why don't you save us all some time and tell us where those missing containers are. You know the ones. You didn't have time to empty your truck out completely into the dumpster behind Rupert's Gas & Auto. But, I presume you noticed they weren't there when you made it back. Well, you are already familiar with Mr. Anderson's dogs, and how well they follow clues. Are you still going to sit there and pretend you're innocent?"

"But … I *am* innocent. And what truck are you talking about? I don't have a truck."

"You're telling us there isn't an older Chevy truck currently parked at your house?" Vance asked. The look on his face said he wasn't buying a word of this, either. "An '81 Chevy Silverado two-tone, namely orange and brown? Ring any bells?"

Jones made an elaborate showing of visibly relaxing. "Oh, *that* truck. It belongs to my dad. You do know he lives with me, don't you?"

"Mm-hmm," Vance said, making some notes into his notebook. "And if we were to send Franco out to your house right now, and bring your father in here, what will he tell us about what he was doing yesterday? Did he, by chance, take his truck for a drive?"

For the first time, a crack appeared in Jones' countenance.

"He, uh, that is to say, my dad wouldn't ... he'd say ..."

"Oh, give it up," Captain Nelson growled. "We know, Jonesy. We know it was you. Don't try to deny it. You're insulting our intelligence with this cockamamie story of yours."

"It's not what you think, sir," Jones finally said. Rivulets of sweat were visible trickling down his forehead.

"Awwooowooo!" Sherlock howled.

"Oooooooo!" Watson added.

Captain Nelson pointed at the dogs, as if to say their vocal objection was all the evidence he needed to lock the officer up and throw away the key.

"There's nothing wrong," Jones insisted, his voice strengthening and growing angry. "I didn't do anything wrong."

"Trespassing, breaking and entering, and theft," Vance said. "As a police officer, I'm sure you know that, when those acts are committed, the local authorities aren't going to take too kindly to such acts."

"Don't forget evading arrest," I added.

Vance snapped his fingers and added the charge to his notebook.

"How long have you been one of my officers?" Captain Nelson suddenly asked.

"Over ten years, sir."

Was it me or did I catch a sneer tagging along with that answer?

"You've been an outstanding cop during that time," the captain continued. "You've had an impeccable record, and are in line to take your sergeant's exams within the next year. Now, would you care to tell me why you put all that in jeopardy, just to steal some bones?"

Jones refused to look at anyone. He sat there, staring into empty space, with a vacant look in his eyes.

"We know you're not covering for anyone," Vance said. "So, help us understand why you did this."

"Like you'd ever understand," Jones snarled.

I held up my hands in a time-out.

"Can I ask a question here?"

The captain nodded his approval.

"Jones, you've been a constant fixture at this police station ever since I moved here. You've always been friendly and polite. In fact, prior to today, I don't think I've ever seen you upset with anyone. Now, I hear the animosity in your voice. You're angry, and if I didn't know any better, I'd say you're angry at the captain, or maybe at the city, or maybe you're just mad at the world, I don't know. But, what I *do* know is this behavior of yours didn't surface until those damn bones did. So, tell me. Is it safe to assume that you are related to Pvt. Darryl Jones, of the 4th OVIR?"

A few seconds passed before Jones finally nodded.

"Can I also assume that you just now, or fairly recently, learned about the history of the SJs?"

Much to my surprise, Jones shook his head no.

"What? You didn't? You mean, you already knew about your ancestor's squad? His history? What happened to him, and so on?"

"I knew about him," Jones said, his voice low. "It's a story I've been told since I was a kid, only I figured it was just that: a story. The one thing I will say is that once I heard an excavation was happening in our city, and it had something to do with the Civil War, I knew. I just knew it had to be about that damn squad. So, I had to check for myself."

"By stealing the artifacts?" Captain Nelson asked. He was doing a good job keeping his voice down, but one look at his face would let anyone know he was beyond furious.

"I had to know it was them," Jones said. "I needed confirmation."

"You're the one who broke into Burt's store!" I exclaimed, snapping my fingers. "You wanted to look through the stuff that was found, didn't you?"

"That was me. I never should have done it."

"Do you have any idea what Burt is going to do to you?" Vance asked. "The man can bench press four hundred and fifty pounds. He's going to snap you in half, like a tooth pick."

"I'll pay for the damage I did. It's my fault. I owe him that."

"What were you looking for?" I asked.

"The sword."

"The sword? The cavalry blade? Why?"

"I needed to know for myself."

"That's something that happened over a hundred-fifty years ago!" Vance insisted. "Why get worked up over it now?"

"Private Jones was the other survivor, wasn't he?" I asked.

"He was, only he wasn't a lowly private. He was the commanding officer."

"What?" Captain Nelson stammered, sitting up in his chair. "Say again?"

"My great-great-grandfather commanded the SJs," Jones said. "The squad chose to follow their commander and deserted their post. It was his decision that forever branded the SJs as deserters."

"The sword," I protested. "We found the initials on the pommel cap. RN. The only soldier with those initials is his ancestor, one Ryan Nelson."

"The sword belonged to Sgt. Darryl Jones," Jones insisted. "I confirmed it when I inspected it myself in that tent."

I looked at Vance. "What am I missing? Why

would the sword be engraved with an RN instead of a DJ?"

"You clearly didn't look hard enough," Jones argued. "And his first name was actually Ryan."

"Then, the engraved letters should have been RJ instead of RN," I insisted.

Captain Nelson looked at Vance. "The sword is still on the table by your office, isn't it?"

"Yes, sir. I asked Franco to watch the table for me. Both the rifle and the sword are there."

"Would you bring the sword here, Detective?"

"Sure thing."

"If there's an RJ on that pommel instead of an RN," I began, shaking my head, "then I think it might be time for an eye exam."

"No offense, Jones," the captain said, after offering me a sly grin, "but if it turns out you're right, and I'm wrong, then it's going to make my family feel a whole lot better."

"I'm sure it would," Jones grumbled. "What about mine? My father thinks his great-grandfather is a mutinous deserter. How do you think that makes my family look?"

"And that's why you took everything," I said. "You want to keep this whole thing under wraps."

"Of course, I do. You may be PV's pretty boy, Anderson, but not all of us have been as fortunate as you."

"Why are you bringing me into this?" I asked, growing defensive. "I didn't do a damn thing here except discover even more human remains on my land. And, for the record, that can stop at any time and you won't hear me complain about it. Hear that, guys? Sherlock? Watson? Stop finding bones on my property."

By now, both of the corgis were snoozing on the floor. Neither one bothered to crack an eye at me during my informal request.

Vance returned, wearing a set of gloves and holding the sword. He held it out to me, hilt first, but not before handing me another pair of gloves. Taking the sword, I held it up to my eyes. There, on the pommel, were two distinct letters: RN. With maybe just a touch of defiance in my eyes, I turned the hilt around so that Jones could see it. Jones, for his part, gave me a slightly pitiful look and leaned forward. Before I knew what he was doing, he used a fingernail to scratch at the letters. Whipping the sword away, I gave him my own scowl before inspecting the sword for damage. What I saw made my heart skip a beat. The top left corner of the N was now missing. Since when does engraved lettering disappear when being scratched by a thumbnail?

"What did you do?" the captain asked.

"I was right," Jones said. "The initials. It's RJ, not RN."

"I saw it for myself," Captain Nelson insisted. "Samuelson and Mr. Anderson also saw the RN. How did you know it was RJ?"

"Because I know the difference between an engraving and a mineral build-up," Jones explained.

"I think I see where he's going with this," I said, after a few moments of silence had passed. Using my own nail, through the glove, I scratched at the N for a few seconds. Deposits of some unknown mineral flaked away as I scratched. Right before my very eyes, the N transformed into a J. What I had failed to realize is that lettering on a sword would be engraved, not raised. I seem to recall originally thinking the second letter was an O.

"It's not an RN?" the captain hopefully asked.

I turned the hilt around to show him. "I was wrong. We all were. Jones is right. Whatever this mineral is that attached itself to the sword, well, it's the same color as the engraved metal. The lettering clearly shows an RJ. That means Darryl Jones was, in fact, Sgt. Darryl Jones. Or Sgt. Ryan Darryl Jones."

Vance consulted his notebook. "Wait. So that means the history books had it wrong, too. They thought O'Henry was in command. Then, thanks to the captain's diary, we thought it was Ryan. Now, we learn it's Darryl?"

Jones looked at the captain with surprise written all over his face. "You have a diary which says your ancestor was in command?"

Captain Nelson was taken aback.

"Well, he specifically didn't say he was in command. I just assumed that, since he was the sole survivor, that he must've been ... Jones, wait. If Ryan Nelson survived the ordeal, and so did

Darryl Jones, then where'd he go? Why didn't he reach out and make himself known?"

At this, Jones hung his head.

"I think we have our answer," I said.

The captain looked at me, with confusion evident on his face.

"Do enlighten us, Mr. Anderson."

"Think about it, sir. The person in charge is Sgt Jones. Against orders, he—and his squad of men —took it upon themselves to relocate to PV. The gold craze was in full swing, and they wanted their share of it, only things didn't go well. They were unable to strike it rich, which meant they had some serious hardships to overcome, hunger being the most prevalent. That diary said that the only thing they found to eat were wild mushrooms? Well, do I need to tell you just how many poisonous varieties exist in nature? I'm thinking they got a bad batch. The only question I have is, was it accidental or intentional?"

We all turned to Officer Jones, who was fidgeting in his chair.

"Got ants in your pants, Jones?" Captain Nelson asked. "Now's the time for clearing your conscience. What do you know about this? Why were those men killed?"

"All I know is what I've been told. Stories, mostly, passed from generation to generation. My great-great-grandfather should never have left Grants Pass. He never should have convinced his men to go with him. What's more, he *hated* seeing his men suffer."

"What's the story?" Vance asked, softening his tone. "What happened that day?"

"I was told Darryl could see that winter was coming. Things were already bad, hunger-wise, so he took it upon himself to go hunting. He packed his gear for several days, but when he returned, he found the entire squad dead."

I pointed at the captain. "What about Ryan? He couldn't have been dead, so where was he?"

"Their commanding officer was gone for several days," Vance repeated, closing his eyes. "The men would still be hungry, and if they'd been surviving off local mushrooms and whatever else they can find, let's just assume they came across a batch of mushrooms they should've left alone. They brewed up another batch of … what, soup? Whatever. Whatever they cooked, the men consumed it, and it killed them. It leads me to believe that Ryan wasn't there at this time. Maybe he was outside? Maybe he was doing the same thing as Darryl and was hunting? Maybe fishing? For whatever the reason, he wasn't there to eat the mushrooms. Returning, he finds everyone dead, panics, and splits."

"Oh, that's just great," Captain Nelson grumbled. "Deserts his men not once, but twice."

"I wonder where he went," I mused.

"He clearly stayed in the area," Vance said. "We already know Ryan Nelson was one of the founding fathers of PV. My question is, why did he let everyone believe he was a sergeant?"

"Maybe he figured since he was the only survivor, that meant he could assume the role of sergeant?" Captain Nelson sighed and pushed back from his desk. "I just don't know why he'd think that. The US Army keeps better records of that."

"Not back then, they didn't," I reminded everyone. "And let's not forget Jones' body wasn't buried in my house's foundation. Nelson should've known there was another survivor, but he didn't. Does that mean the two of them went their separate ways?"

"Maybe Nelson *thought* Jones was dead," Vance suggested. "Yes, it's a guess, but then again, that's all anyone can do at this point: guess. Look what happened. We all thought someone completely different was in command. Turns out, none of us were right. Well, except for Jones."

"My ancestor was a deserter," Jones scoffed. He looked at the captain. "Turns out, so was yours. History is not going to look kindly on us."

I don't know what prompted me to speak right then, and even so, I was surprised by the boldness of what came out.

"It will if none of this comes to light."

The office fell silent. Captain Nelson, Officer Jones, and Vance all stared at me. I sighed, reached out to Vance, and pointed at his notebook. "May I? Good. Now, look. History already has got it wrong. Who says we have to change it? Captain, why don't you put that diary away? Vance, what would happen if you lose your notes to this case? And Jones, so far, there's no harm done, provided you return those bones."

"What are you going to do with them?" Jones asked, in a sullen voice.

"I'm going to reach out to the university and let them have 'em," I answered. "I'll leave it up to them if they'd like to try and find descendants. If they can, great, they can be properly buried. If not, then the university says they'll take care of them. Study them, I guess. As for the artifacts, well, I've since changed my mind about keeping anything. I'm all for letting Burt and his antique store sell whatever they want. Vance, Captain, you each wanted a rifle? They're yours. Jones, this sword rightfully belongs to you. If you don't want it, I think the captain would like it. Otherwise, you can do with it whatever you want. Hey, for the record, why *did* you steal those bones?"

"Deserters don't deserve a decent burial."

"Everyone does, whether you believe it or not," I argued. "Besides, how can you possibly know what happened over a hundred years ago? Talk about extenuating circumstances. Besides, the men were simply following orders. You can be mad at your ancestor if you choose, but don't deny his men a proper burial just because you don't approve."

"Mr. Anderson is right," Captain Nelson said. "What's done is done. There's no need for this to go any further. Jones? Will you tell us where to find the missing bones?"

JEFFREY POOLE

"And no one has to know I had any part in the theft?" Jones asked. A ray of hope had appeared in the officer's voice.

We all turned to the captain, who was silent as he considered. Finally, after two minutes had passed without anyone uttering a word, he rose to his feet and held out a hand.

"What happened in this room can stay in this room. Jonesy? Don't you have something to be doing?"

Gratitude washed over Jones' face. He started to nod. After a few moments, he pointed straight down.

"They're down there."

Me, Vance, the captain, and my two dogs—who had woken up during Jones' outburst—craned our necks to look at the floor.

"You buried them?" Vance asked, confused.

"What's down there?" I asked. "A basement?"

The captain snapped his fingers and gave Jones' an appraising stare.

"The evidence room, located in the basement. You simply added those boxes to our own, is that it?"

"He pulled an Ark of the Covenant on us, didn't he?" Vance said, impressed.

"How big of a basement does this place have?" I demanded.

Jones grinned, nodded once at the captain, and exited the office.

EPILOGUE

T his is so exciting! I don't think I'm going to be able to wait until it's done. I mean, just think of it. This will be our home! A home that we both designed, together. You're excited, aren't you?"

"You can't hear it, but inside, I'm jumping up and down and screaming like a little girl," I told my wife, giving her hand a squeeze. "The old foundation is finally gone and the new one is already in place. I mean, look at it. Good grief, it's huge! Did we screw up and order a place that was too big for the two of us?"

"Don't second guess yourself now, dear," Jillian giggled. She inserted her arm through mine and, together, we walked along the huge concrete slab that was the beginning of our new mansion.

I pointed at a smaller slab on the left that looked as though it had been added as an afterthought.

"What's this over here? Did we make an expansion and I simply forgot?"

"I do believe that's the garage, Zachary."

"The garage? This whole thing? You're kidding."

The slab, I should point out, was bigger than Aunt Bonnie's old house, and my old house in Phoenix, Arizona, combined. Seriously, from the looks of the thing, I could easily park a dozen cars in there and have room for more. I looked at Jillian and gave an exasperated shake of my head.

"When the world runs out of concrete, they'll know who's to blame."

"Oh, Zachary. Don't be melodramatic. The garage is only designed to hold four cars."

"I figured. Four for you, and four for me. I get it, it's a lot of space."

Jillian giggled and swatted my arm. She then led me over to an offshoot of the main foundation, extending south. This one's function, I'm thankful to say, was easy to determine. There, running nearly twenty-five feet across and at least twice that in length, was … let's call it an indentation. I mean, anyone looking at it can see that it's going to be a pool. An indoor pool. Wow. I just love saying that.

Sorry, I'm getting side-tracked.

"I still don't understand Officer Jones' motivation," Jillian was saying, as we slowly walked around the perimeter of the future pool. "Why did he do it? According to you, the captain, and even Officer Jones, no one really knew what had happened to those men, right?"

"That's right. It wasn't until the bones were

discovered did past childhood stories come back to haunt him. He had to know if what he heard was true."

"And once he knew?" Jillian asked. "What then?"

"Well, as soon as he knew that the final resting place for his ancestor's old squad of men had been located, he knew that there was a chance for even more dirt to be flung at his family. So, he did what any moronic idiot would have done without thinking things through: he panicked and stole all the items. Oh, and this is after he burglarized Burt's shop. I hear he's still trying to work up the nerve to apologize to him. Can't say I blame him. That's the last guy on the planet that I would want mad at me. Anyway, Jones didn't want to fuel any more rumors that his family was known for its mutinous ways."

"So, how did the bones end up buried in your foundation?"

I chuckled, took my wife's hand, and started back.

"Can't wait to see how the stage is going to look. Okay, you asked about the hidden bones. Well, we did some more digging. Me and Vance. Now that we knew what to look for, and which names to research, it went a little easier. In this case, Pfc Ryan Nelson got some schooling and became an architect. Or an engineer, I'm not sure which. At any rate, he must've kept an eye on that abandoned barn, because one day, and it's not clear how it started, part of the barn burned down."

"Oh, no! Was anyone hurt?"

"No. Well, Ryan Nelson might've had a heart attack, but aside from that, I don't think anyone was hurt. I found mention of the town's decision to just tear down the barn, but Ryan managed to convince them that the foundation was still good, and the new owners of the property should consider using it as the foundation for their new home. It'd be a great way to save money, he said."

"What year was this?" Jillian wanted to know.

"1910. I can only imagine that, by this time, Ryan had snuck back to the site of the original encampment and walled it in, making it look like it was nothing more than a continuation of the foundation. So, when the new owners took over, they followed Ryan's instructions and, to save a few bucks, they built their house over the old foundation and the burial site of SJ squad."

"That's right. You said Bonnie's house was built in 1911."

"I did," I confirmed.

"And Ryan was still alive? I wonder how old he was."

"Well, let's figure, as a private, he would have been in his early twenties. The year was in the mid-1860s. Fifty years later, he would have been in his seventies. Yeah, that's still doable."

We heard the blast of a horn and immediately looked north, toward town. There was no mistake what was currently headed down the road: trucks. From the sounds of it, *big* trucks.

"Could it be something for the house?" Jillian asked.

"That's what I'm thinking. And ... we're right. Jillian! Check it out! Wow. Get a load of that, er, load!"

Three full-sized semis, hauling flatbeds loaded with all manner of wood products, were approaching our drive. The first two were hauling several stacks of a variety of trusses, while the third had two-by-fours, two-by-sixes, and a few sizes I didn't know were even available. The first truck reached our driveway and turned. Within moments, I had three huge trucks approaching the site, with two stuck on my driveway, as the first figured out how—and where—he was supposed to deposit his load. Thankfully, a few workers were still here from the construction crew.

I let them determine where everything was going to go. While the truck set up a mini-crane, that was evidently built into the cargo trailer, I steered Jillian toward far southern corner of the foundation, which was where our master bedroom was going to be.

"Have you given much thought about the second Ireland book?" Jillian wanted to know.

I let out a sigh, and it must've been louder than I had anticipated.

"Oooh, it's that bad, huh? I'm sorry, Zachary. You know, it's okay to tell Vance and Tori no. There's no pressure on you, and you have nothing to prove. You're a wonderful writer, and I couldn't be happier for you. Or prouder."

Smiling, I pulled her in for a hug.

"Thanks. I want to write this book, I really do, it's just that … well, I'm having trouble figuring out the overall theme to the story. Tori's character has so much spirit that I …"

"What is it?" Jillian asked, as she noticed I had trailed off and now a vacant look had come over my features. "Earth to Zachary, Earth to Zachary, are you there?"

I blinked a few times. Of course! Why hadn't I seen it before? It was perfect! I could make this work!

"Spirit!" I exclaimed.

"Okay, what about it?" Jillian cautiously asked.

"The *Spirit of Éire*! I can't believe I didn't think of it before!"

"Is that the name of the new book?"

"It's going to be," I said, growing excited. I reached into my back pocket for my own personal notebook. "Of course, of course. This time, she'll take Ireland with her, on her journey to America. I can have her reflect on her decision to leave her home country, which she loves very much. But, having survived the ordeal of the Great Famine, she knows she has to do what's best for her family. So, what does she do? The same thing everyone else has been forced to do, which is leave the country. She wants to start a new life in a new home. Where is she going to find that new home? Right here, in the good ol' US of A."

Jillian was silent as she studied my face.

"What is it?" I asked. "Food in the tooth or bat in the cave?"

My wife burst out laughing and she swatted my arm again.

"You know I don't like that analogy."

"Makes you laugh though. Seriously, though. What do you think?"

"I think you have the makings of another bestseller on your hands. Are you going to tell Vance and Tori that you've thought of an idea?"

"Not just yet. I want to flesh this out first, but this certainly feels right, like … like …"

"It's what should logically happen next for the story," Jillian finished for me.

"Exactly."

The semis finished unloading their cargo and managed to get their rigs turned around. The three of them hadn't been gone for more than five minutes when we heard the approach of yet another car. This one was a van, and it had a big "11" on the side of it.

"What are they doing here?" Jillian asked, growing concerned. "There's nothing for them to … Zachary? Did you call them?"

"I did. I owe Clara Springfield an interview. It was in exchange for leaving us alone while the professor worked his archaeological magic."

Jillian took the leashes from me, gave me a quick kiss, and headed for her car.

"You have fun on your interview. The dogs and

I will be heading home. I'm so very glad we drove separately. What should we do when we make it home? Maybe put a movie on? How long do you think you'll be? Oh, never mind. I know you won't mind watching the new Sandra Bullock romance movie."

"You're killing me, Smalls," I moaned. "Thanks a lot, Judas."

"Love you!" Jillian called, as she hurriedly loaded the dogs into her SUV. Slipping behind the wheel, my lovely wife practically peeled out as she rushed by the arriving van.

I stood there, motionless, as I watched the reporter exit the van, help prepare the camera, and then made sure she was presentable. She saw me standing nearby, nudged her driver/cameraman, and started walking my way.

"Thank you for keeping your promise, Mr. Anderson."

"A deal is a deal," I returned. "Let's get started, shall we?"

All through the interview, I could safely say my mind was elsewhere. In fact, now that I knew how I was going to handle the new Ireland book, I was already setting up the story in my head. Who says I can't multitask?

While my thoughts were literally thousands of miles away, at this very moment, certain events were being set into motion that would directly affect me and my wonderfully quiet lifestyle here in the Pacific Northwest. In approximately six weeks, I was going to get a phone call that would not only persuade me to get on a plane, but it would also have me bringing along Jillian *and* my two dogs. Just where would we be going? Well, that would be to a place I had absolutely no plans on visiting. Ever.

We were going to be heading to the Arctic. Oh, joy.

AUTHOR'S NOTE

You wouldn't think a Pacific Northwest state like Oregon would have played that much of a role in our country's Civil War, so imagine my surprise when I looked it up, expecting absolutely *nada* and I found quite a lengthy history on my state's role. Granted, it wasn't the biggest part in the play, but there were military forts and bases everywhere. And no, there wasn't a post, or a fort, in Grants Pass. But, believe it or not, there were over twenty-five posts scattered throughout the territory that had just recently become a state. Thank you, Wikipedia.

With regards to the actual Oregonian soldiers in the Civil War, let me just say that no, there was no 4th Oregon Voluntary Infantry Regiment. It didn't exist, obviously. I found instances of a 1st, possibly a 2nd, but it stops there.

The Enemy Never Came: The Civil War in the Pacific Northwest is a real book, but obviously does not contain any information about my imaginary regiment.

All right, what's next for Zack and the dogs? Well, as I briefly mentioned at the end of the epilogue, a trip up north is in the works. Zack is going to learn that there is only a select few emperor penguin breeding facilities scattered across the globe. Being in dire need of more qualified institutions to help preserve the threatened penguins, Zack and the gang are formally asked to lend their expertise when a new facility opens and some of their penguins turn up missing! For you fans of fantasy, I'm also hard at work on the return to Lentari, with Blast from the Past (ToL#10). A former villain has resurfaced and has completely changed the Kingdom of Lentari, only, not in a good way.

That's it for now. Please, don't forget to leave a (hopefully good!) review wherever you purchased the book. Those reviews enable us to be found that much quicker whenever someone is looking for a new book.

Until next time! Happy reading!

J.
June, 2022

Zack and the dogs will be back in their next adventure,
Case of the Unlucky Emperor **(Corgi Case Files #17)!**

**Meanwhile, catch up on the entire
Corgi Case Files Series**
Available in e-book and paperback

Case of the One-Eyed Tiger
Case of the Fleet-Footed Mummy
Case of the Holiday Hijinks
Case of the Pilfered Pooches
Case of the Muffin Murders
Case of the Chatty Roadrunner
Case of the Highland House Haunting
Case of the Ostentatious Otters
Case of the Dysfunctional Daredevils
Case of the Abandoned Bones
Case of the Great Cranberry Caper
Case of the Shady Shamrock
Case of the Ragin' Cajun
Case of the Missing Marine
Case of the Stuttering Parrot
Case of the Rusty Sword

If you enjoy Epic Fantasy, check out Jeff's other series:
Pirates of Perz
Tales of Lentari
Bakkian Chronicles
(all coming out in new releases from
Secret Staircase Books in 2023!)

60171842R00156